DARKENED
HOLLOWS

Also by Gary Lee Vincent

Novels
PASSAGEWAY
DARKENED HILLS

Nonfiction
THE WINNER, THE LOSER
AGELATIONS
SURVIVING THE SWINE FLU
CONFIGURATION MANAGEMENT

Musical Releases
100 PERCENT
PASSION, PLEASURE, & PAIN
SOMEWHERE DOWN THE ROAD

DARKENED HOLLOWS

GARY LEE VINCENT

Burning Bulb
PUBLISHING

Darkened Hollows
By **Gary Lee Vincent**

Burning Bulb Publishing
P.O. Box 4721
Bridgeport, WV 26330-4721
www.BurningBulbPublishing.com

Copyright © 2011 Gary Lee Vincent. All rights reserved.
Cover designed by Gary Lee Vincent.
Incubus image © FotoWorx – Fotolia.com; used under license.
Tunnel of life image © Melinda Nagy – Fotolia.com; used under license.
Bergbau image © Albert Schleich – Fotolia.com; used under license.

Edition ISBN

Paperback 978-0-61552-722-2

First edition.
Printed in the United States of America.

Library of Congress Control Number: 2011936498

Dedicated to:

My lovely wife Carla and
my beautiful daughter Amber Lee.

INTRODUCTION

True evil never dies, it just changes shape. I should have realized this when opening the proverbial Pandora's Box with *Darkened Hills*. I should have. Did I really believe that I could just tell the story and leave it? I suppose I did.

However, even as I finished penning the first installment of *DARKENED: The West Virginia Vampire Series*, *Darkened Hills* didn't die, it growled.

Oh yes, it could have been bigger, but when the dark forces grab you by the throat, hold you straight to the task of writing until it's finished, you enjoy a small breath of fresh air; a moment to stop and quickly back away before the story possesses you with its evil.

That illusion of relief is short lived, as it would appear we need to continue this journey we've started, traveling down its damned path to see what really happened in those *Darkened Hills* and to do that, we need to dig down – down into the *Darkened Hollows*.

Well, here's the rest of it (for now at least)...

ACKNOWLEDGEMENTS

With projects such as these, they could not be possible without the support of several folks whom I'd like to acknowledge here.

First off, I would like to thank the fans who supported me with the purchase of *Darkened Hills* and for helping to make it *ForeWord Reviews Magazine's* *"Book of the Year"* for the best horror novel by an independent press in 2010.

A kind regards goes out to fellow horror novelist Rich Bottles Jr., whom I work with almost daily and has been there since the first installment of the *DARKENED* series. I appreciated his help in proofreading the story and for listening to me explain the various plot strategies, just so that I could hear how they sounded before they got to paper.

I would like to thank the novelist Kelly R. Martin who also helped with the proofreading of this work.

I would like to thank Linda Innes for her editorial contributions in keeping Book II on target with schedule and content.

Finally, a warm appreciation goes out to my family who had to live with me throughout this book's development.

PROLOGUE

Jeff Abraham sat in a six foot by six-foot jail cell in Huttonsville Correctional Center pondering as he did every day, just how in the hell he wound up here.

He thought he had a pretty good life; that was until his wife was killed. For Jeff, life consisted of working as Vice President of the Empire National Bank, processing rather mundane requests for loans, business accounts, and the like, and then going out with his friends for an occasional round of golf.

One morning, Jeff arrived home to find a police car parked in his driveway. Jeff, who had been out on one of his out-of-town golf trips, did not have a convincing enough alibi to support the carnage they discovered in the Abraham residence.

Their elegant house on Walnut Grove was trashed. In fact, one of the golfers at the Walnut Grove Golf Course called authorities when he noticed smoke coming from the kitchen.

The smoke was caused by some food that had been left in the oven too long. However, when the fire department came to investigate, they noticed that there was blood throughout the living room and much of the furniture had been knocked over.

Although the body was never discovered, a jury was persuaded enough to believe that Jeff Abraham killed his wife. He was sentenced to twenty years in Huttsonville.

That was eighteen months ago.

As Jeff stared at the walls, daydreaming about his beautiful wife Jillian, a person tapped on the cell door.

"Mr. Abraham," it was Warden Smith. "I have some good news."

"Really?" Jeff asked, skeptical.

"There was a house fire in Melas," Warden Smith continued, "Your wife's remains were discovered in the basement.

"The coroner could not determine the exact time of death, but believes that she died in the fire which was, let's see here," the warden flipped through some papers he was holding, "six months ago and not a year and a half ago as was previously thought."

Almost smugly, Warden Smith added, "I guess since you were locked up here during that time there was no way you could have murdered her."

Jeff jumped to his feet and ran over to the door to face the warden. "I told you I was innocent! My life, my career – all ruined – because no one would believe me!"

"Everybody who comes here says they're innocent, son," Warden Smith countered. "We figured that if a jury convicts a man, then he must be guilty. I guess it's your lucky day."

"So I get to go home now?" Jeff asked.

"Sure," the warden replied. "But I'd like you to stop by Reggie McCoy's office before you're released. He'll try to help make your reintegration into society as smooth as possible."

***

Reggie McCoy was a large black man that weighed around 300 pounds and set behind a typical government-issued wooded desk smoking a cigarillo as he leafed through Jeff Abraham's release paperwork. Jeff wondered how this man could find anything in his office. Looking around, he was amazed at how cluttered it was.

The place was littered with stacks of binders and folders containing reports just like his report that Reggie was looking at now. Some of these records were standing in paper 'towers' raising three feet or more from a spot on the floor where they stood. In fact, it was almost as if every horizontal surface in Reggie McCoy's office, with the exception of a small path to the desk, had something placed in it.

Jeff thought that at any moment, the cigarillo would set one of the paper stacks on fire and the whole prison would have to be evacuated.

"Man, you's a lucky son-of-a-bitch," Reggie said with a smile that showed a full set of yellowing teeth.

"Why the fuck you say that!" Jeff said with disgust. "I shouldn't been thrown into this hell hole to begin with!"

"I'm just saying that at least you got justice. That would have sucked had you not gotten off until your term was up."

"Yea, I suppose you're right," Jeff replied. "You have a way of cheering a fellow up."

"That I do," Reggie replied, grinning again. "I also have something else that might cheer you up!" He ruffled through some of the papers on his desk and pulled out a form, "Here it is."

"You be from Melas, West Virginia, right?" Reggie asked.

"Yes, I am *from* Melas," Jeff replied, somewhat disgusted at Reggie McCoy's grammar skills.

"Well, since you've been in jail, most of the town has been – shit man, how's I'm going to tell ya this?" He scratched his head, trying to come up with an appropriate description to Melas turning into a ghost town. "Um, most of the town had been shut down."

He studied Jeff's face, which showed no real sign of acknowledging what Reggie was trying to convey – that no one lived in Melas anymore. Reggie thought it best he move on to a different subject. "Anyway, the state has a new work-release program with Cassie Coal in which we place our inmates into full time jobs when they get out."

"I was a bank vice president before I got here, what does this have to do with me?" Jeff asked.

"Well, since you're a convicted felon most places won't want to hire you." Reggie held up a hand to block off an expected protest. "Yes, Jeff, I know you innocent and all, but I'm just saying that if you go under this program, you won't have to hit the streets out of work, and all. You hear me, man?"

"Yes," Jeff replied. "I hear you."

"Good," Reggie said. "Cassie Coal has some openings over at their Dark Hollow Mine near Melas. Since that is where your house is, it won't be too far from home."

"I thought that mine was closed down." Jeff said.

"I'm not a businessman, Jeff," Reggie replied. "So, do you want a job or not?"

***

Preston Hunt was a land surveyor and General Partner with Hunt-Wilson Engineering Group. He sat in his Jeep and reviewed his latest request.

In his hands, he held a work order from Cassie Coal Company as they had recently acquired a 240-acre partial that ran from Raccoon Run Road to Dark Hollow Road. The Raccoon Run portion cut into a piece of what used to be the town of Melas, but now Melas for the most part was a ghost town.

A large section of homes on Raccoon Run Road appeared to have been destroyed, as if some fire had came through and gutted them all. A fire had gutted this area about a year earlier. Preston did not know the town's evil history or the events that led up to that fateful night in which the blaze occurred.

A few minutes earlier, he placed the westernmost survey stake on the top of a hill where the Madison House once stood. Now, only charred remains were left of the former mansion. A lonely chimney rose tall above the flat where an impressive estate once imposed its presence over the town of Melas below.

That stake took the property line from the top of the ridge down to the second stake located at 1279 Raccoon Run Road. This was the only house that survived the blaze. It looked isolated and very much alone in the forest of weeds and charred overgrowth.

Preston parked the Jeep and got out to figure out where to setup his equipment.

The letters "W.M. Murray" could barely be read on a soot-covered mailbox that also somehow survived the blaze.

What didn't survive the blaze was a burnt-up Ford Explorer in the driveway. The Explorer looked like it might have been white at one time, but now was a charred, blackened heap.

Preston found it quite curious that a large stone was on the Explorer's hood, almost like it had been set there as an anchor to keep it from magically driving away. "How in the hell did that get there?" he wondered to himself.

As he approached the Explorer to get a better look at the stone, he noticed that directly in front of the vehicle were several other stones, much smaller, but of the same kind of rock the bigger stone was made of.

He noticed that, although charred, the stones appeared to be engraved with some type of hieroglyphics. Preston's first thought was that some kind of meteor or alien ship had crash-landed into this hill, burning everything, and here were its remains.

Well, take that back, it burnt up everything except the stones, the mailbox, and the house.

Contemplating the bizarre scene before him, Preston thought he saw one of the stones move. He blinked his eyes and the stone looked like it was in the same place as before.

Preston walked over to what appeared to be the center of the rock heap. There were stones of various sizes and all seemed to have the strange markings on them. He climbed up on top of the rocks to have a closer look.

Standing there, he thought he heard a slight humming noise. As he stood quietly, listening for the sound, he realized that ever since he started the survey, he had not heard much of anything, even a bird or dog. The hill was terribly quiet; quiet that was, except for the soft hum.

One of the rocks underfoot moved. Preston looked down, curious to see if the rock simply shifted from him standing on the pile or if it truly was moving.

"This is absurd," Preston thought to himself. "Stones do not move on their own."

The humming noise grew louder and was followed by a soft vibration in the ground. Preston stared at his feet. This time saw a small stone move.

The stone was about the size of a baseball, so Preston decided to reach down and pick it up. The material looked like marble and Preston fully expected it to be heavy, hard, and porous - like a rock.

The stone felt cold to the touch, icy in fact. This was strange to Preston, because it was late August. The stone also was soft and felt like putty in his hands.

He made a fist with the hand holding the rock and was able to squeeze it, as if it were soft clay.

Before his very eyes, the rock and his hand were one. Although he felt no pain initially, he stared in disbelief as he brought his left hand up to his eyes to see that it was solid stone.

"My God!" Preston exclaimed. "What's going on!"

Suddenly, other stones began to move. Those underfoot sucked his legs into them like they were quicksand. Preston let out a scream, acutely aware that his voice was the only voice that could be heard on the hillside.

Three days later, search crews located Preston Hunt's Jeep on Raccoon Run Road. The county authorities towed both it and the abandoned Explorer off the property and into town for examination. As the Explorer was wrenched up onto the flatbed tow truck, the large rock on the hood simply rolled off and landed at the foot of an obelisk.

Dan Tomas, the tow truck driver, scratched his head and wondered who in the world drive their car into a stone monument. "Probably a bunch of vandals," he thought. Dan assumed that this was a marker for a forgotten cemetery.

As he pulled away, the yard did not have any more stones, only an obelisk with its top broken off and lying next to it.

Preston Hunt was never seen or heard from again.

CHAPTER 1

Stan O'Donnel was the Harrison County Sheriff at the time the animals started being killed. As he carefully navigated one of the county's few police cruisers over a snow-covered U.S. Route 50 freeway that November morning, he regretted that Jim Jackson was still in the hospital.

"Jimmy's Ford Bronco would probably do better than this Crown Vic," Stan told his partner Todd McCoy as they approached the turnoff toward Melas.

"It would have, had he not rolled it," Todd replied smugly.

A couple weeks earlier, Deputy Jackson was investigating a boy's death at the Melas Industrial Home For Troubled Youth when he was hit by an oncoming car that had ran a stop sign. Jackson was traveling just fast enough that his vehicle rolled and Jackson himself was ejected from the cabin.

"You know, Stan," Todd said out of the blue, "this town kind of creeps me out."

Stan guffawed from deep in his throat, a gesture indicating that he somewhat agreed with Todd, but would not freely admit it.

As they drove down Main Street, they noticed that several of the businesses had shut down: Rothenstein and Pinkman's Coin Shoppe – closed, Wagner's Grocery Store – closed, the Dairy Queen – closed for the winter, but from the looks of the ice cream-shaped road sign blown off and lying in the snow-covered parking lot, it might stay closed.

"I hope you're not hungry this morning, Todd," Stan said as they drove by the restaurant.

"Well, I'd probably pass on ice cream this morning anyway," Todd replied.

The two made their way through town and onto Dark Hollow Road. They were on their way to see Abner Wagner, a local farmer and brother to Bo Wagner, who owned the recently-closed Wagner's Grocery.

Brother Bo was found the same morning that James Jackson wrecked his car, in fact just down the block from it. Bo was on Main Street naked and running from a state police officer who was about to question him for public lewdness when Bo 'tripped' when the officer hit him in the back with his police baton, and busted his head on a newspaper vending machine.

Wagner's Grocery was never reopened after Bo died. Brother Abner may have tried to get the store back up, but distanced himself after health inspectors found unsanitary conditions in their meat department.

10

As Abner's main source of income was his livestock, he could not afford to be associated with tainted meat.

In any case, Abner Wagner was in a panic this morning and frantically paced on his porch as the officers pulled into his driveway.

"Boys, what took you so long?" Abner yelled, coming down from the porch to meet them.

"Calm down," Stan replied. "Roads are getting bad, looks like winter is coming early this year."

"Damn coal trucks is what's fucking up the road, I tell you!" Abner said, with obvious resentment in his voice. "They'll have this whole place undermined in a decade, mark my words."

"Well, Mr. Wagner," Todd protested, "everything is slicker than a cat's ass, not just Dark Hollow."

The aging farmer seemed not to want to argue and changed the subject. "I'll have Kelly get you boys some coffee in a minute, but what I need to show you can't wait!"

Without waiting for the men to get close enough to even shake hands, Abner Wagner turned and made a semicircle around the porch and headed towards his barn, just to the rear of the residence.

"You say something's attacked your animals?" Todd yelled out to Abner. The two lawmen looked at each other and quickened their pace to hurry and catch up with the farmer.

"I could tell you, but it's better that I show you!" Abner replied. The three men waded through about six inches of snow-covered earth.

Stan pulled out a notebook and cursed under his breath as his pen looked like it had frozen up from the cold. "Todd, see if you have a pen that works," he commanded. "And make note of those tracks, while you're at it."

One thing that Stan could notice right away was there were only one set of footprints leading from the house to the barn, then back again. These were probably the farmer's.

As the men stood before the barn door, Abner Wager looked like a man who was both shaken and infuriated. His face was red and his gray hair jutted out from a red Massey Ferguson cap the farmer was wearing.

"You boys had better find out who did this!" Abner exclaimed, throwing open the barn door.

Inside, the barn was empty.

Todd shrugged his shoulders and looked around. "I don't see anything out of the ordinary," he said.

"It's not here," Abner said, "but just behind the barn, in the pin."

As the three men crossed through the confines of the barn, they could see out into an enclosed field just beyond the barn's threshold. Looking at the pin beyond was surreal, as if a different scene was staged inside the frame of the barn's rear door and the men stood looking through a frame at a picture before them.

There – out in the snow-covered field – were heaps of something that from a distance appeared like piles of dirty laundry.

As they approached, the piles were not laundry at all, but the carcasses of hogs that Abner raised. The animals lay lifeless in the snow.

Stan noticed a peculiarity about the first hog he came to. "Todd, give me a hand with this, will you?"

The two police officers moved the hog around to see that its throat had been slashed – or at least it looked that way, as there was a crimson stain that resembled a cut that went from ear to ear.

"They're all like that!" Abner hollered in a loud, distraught voice. All eight of them!"

Stan gave a grave glance to Todd as he inspected the wound on the animal's neck. The wound was not a cut, but some sort of puncture or bite.

Besides the minute amount of crimson that stained the hog's neck, Todd verbalized what Stan was observing. "There's no blood."

"That's right." Abner acknowledged. "They're all like that! No fucking blood in any of em!" The farmer spit on the ground in disgust. A brown tobacco spit stain marred the ever-white snow.

"Write this in your notes, Todd," Stan said. "Eight hog cadavers with throat traumas. Cause of death: exsanguination."

Todd wasn't the brightest bulb in the ceiling and as he struggled with the spelling of 'exsanguination,' the sheriff shook his head and immediately regretted using a four-dollar word with the deputy.

Stan quickly changed the subject and addressed Abner, "You said Kelly has some coffee brewing back at the house?"

"Yes, sir, Sheriff," the farmer replied.

"Good. Let's get out of the cold and discuss this matter further. Todd, you go grab the camera out of the cruiser and take some shots, will you? When you are finished, meet us in Abner's kitchen."

"Sure thing, boss," Todd replied. "Just be sure to save me some coffee."

***

After meeting with the farmer and his wife, the two police officers set in quiet for several minutes during their ride back to Clarksburg.

Eventually, it was Todd who broke the silence. "So, who do you think's doing it?"

"Who, or *what*, you mean," Stan replied.

"This is all very odd," Todd continued. "This is the third case like this this month. Farmers are going to start panicking; demanding answers."

"Answers we don't have," Stan mused, "at least not yet anyway."

"Well I'm convinced it's probably some punk-ass kids, probably on drugs. There's nothing for them around here. Hell, just look at Melas – that place is a ghost town. With no opportunity, kids get into trouble or they move out of state and start a life elsewhere."

"I don't know, Todd," Stan rebutted. "It just doesn't add up. I mean, if it were only one animal, or so, then yeah, maybe some hellions did it." He shook his head, "Heck, back when I was a kid, the worse things anyone ever did was cow tipping."

Todd laughed. "You're sounding old dude and you're only what, forty? Tell me, did you have to walk through a foot of snow when you were in grade school?"

"Nope," Stan replied, "I'm not *that* old! When it snowed that deep, schools were cancelled."

Just then, the CB radio kicked on alerting the officers to respond to an accident on Rt. 50 in Wilsonburg. They were close."

"Look's like it's going to be a busy day," Todd said.

"It appears that way," Stan replied.

***

Later that night, an exhausted Stan O'Donnel made his way to the evidence room. Something about this morning's animal case bugged him.

He began looking through pictures of the various animals that had been killed. Each had two very small puncture wounds on their necks. The earlier pictures from October were messier, but in all cases the animals were drained of their blood.

"The perp is getting better as time goes on," he said to himself.

He pulled out a county map and began making marks representing the various farms that had been hit. All of the farms were in the western part of the county, with Tarklin flanking the westernmost point and Wolf Summit on the east. In the dead center was Melas.

Melas. James Jackson's old stomping ground.

Melas – the town where just last month the Dicklands were brutally murdered in a robbery. Or was it a robbery?

Stan got up and retrieved the case file on the Dickland murders. It was the most recent in a string of bad things going down in Melas, animal killings excluded.

The Dicklands owned a candy store. The husband had been decapitated and his body left in the store's dumpster. The wife had been killed with bite marks on her wrist and neck.

"Bite marks," Stan said.

In his heart of hearts, Stan O'Donnel felt that whoever committed the candy story murders was the same perpetrator doing the animal killings. Unlike his deputy, Stan disagreed with the assessment that the perp was some kids jacked up on a drug-induced frenzy. No, the Sheriff truly believed they were dealing with a vampire. "No one is going to believe me, so I best keep it quiet," he said to himself.

Despite the fact that he already worked a twelve-hour shift and he had promised to take his girlfriend out for a steak dinner after work, Stan continued working throughout the night and clear into the next morning, pulling everything he could on the town of Melas.

CHAPTER 2

The Clarksburg Reporter
SERIAL KILLER
WHILDERS TRANSCRIPT RELEASED

MELAS – On October 2, the area was stunned by the revelation of a story that had been years in the making and almost completely unnoticed by the local community.

Now the public gets a chance to read the story, told by James "Jimbo" Whilders himself.

The transcript was taken from audio recordings that Childers delivered to police the same day he took his own life.

Investigators released transcripts of the taped confession of James Whilders Wednesday morning.

Whilders describes his confession as an insight into what makes a killer a killer.

In addition to a killing spree that spanned over a decade, the Melas handyman also claims vampires compelled him to carry out their deeds. However, he personally admitted to murdering six women and an undisclosed number of men; disposing their bodies in a deep mine shaft in the abandoned Runners Ridge coal mine before killing himself at the Townehouse Motor Lodge three weeks ago.

The remains of Shirley Volkwien were found near the entrance of the dangerous mine. According to Whilders' cryptic message on the tape, the bodies of twenty-three other women remain and if the vampire tale is to be believed, possibly more.

The remains of Mary Jenn Parker were found in Whilders' house in Melas on North Coat Drive, just south of U.S. Route 50 in Harrison County.

In addition to the disposing some of the bodies in the mines, the remains of other victims may have been burned in a series of arsons that occurred last year near Whilders' residence on North Coat Drive.

These descriptions are not clear and because of the dangerous conditions in the mines, investigators have called off the search for those remaining.

Whilders described his victims as "hookers," but investigators are unclear if the women were in fact prostitutes or transients from outside the area. To date, no missing persons report has been filed on any of the victims, thus complicating the investigation.

You can read the complete transcript of his confession below. The transcript does include offensive language and random thoughts from the killer…

TRANSCRIPTION

JW: James B. Whilders

JW: Okay, I'm going to write a note about what happened and then I'm also going to record this, so, make sure that the police get what they need. All right. Like I said, my name is James Bogart Whilders.

JW: I burned all those houses down on North Coat Street and my brother's friend Talman Cane – TC as we called him – helped me.

JW: TC was like my lookout there. And Walter Pinkman also helped me watch the front of the house, make sure nobody was there. But I'm pissed off at Walt because he hollered too late and he didn't give me enough time to get away. I almost got caught by the fucking police. Cause, uhm, a police officer – Jackson was his name – stopped me up there on Jacobs Street.

JW: That's the same cop I had talked to from a previous fire. I thought he had me. I mean he had

19

pulled right up on me with his Bronco and uh, he had his light, side light shining on me and I said, well, I'm in a rush and got to get home.

JW: So, he didn't think nothing of it and I got away with it. Fuck, I had matches in my pocket.

JW: Alright, so I went home to listen to the sirens from the fire trucks. I stayed put in my house during the fire, and they fight it, it's out. But the impotency of the Melas Police Department with that arson investigation was appalling to say the least.

JW: Walt had pussy at home waiting on him, he wanted to get home, back home to it. Mina was her name. He had to get home to Mina. I don't know how that old bastard did it. Mina was his niece. She was a fine-looking piece of ass. I think he was banging his niece, that's probably what gave him the stroke.

[laughs]

JW: So anyway, uhm-

JW: Those cats in the, the police department were clueless. You could tell by the way they handled that operation.

JW: But, anyway, early on we had to burn the houses down.   See, that's where the first few were killed. Hell, we had to burn up the evidence.

JW: When Walt first hired me for the job, he clearly stated that each of the bodies had to have their heads chopped off.   TC agreed with him. I tell you what, Walt was a sick old fool who was nuts and I had to be nuts to go along with him.

JW: Aah, but the money was good and Walt kept his end of the deal. I'd go out, pick up the hookers, rough them up and drop them off at that old abandoned house up on the hill – Madison House. I always had to bring them around to the back. Walt and TC would take the girls from there and meet me back at the chopping block on North Coat when they were finished.

JW: I don't know what those fuckers were doing with those girls, but when they brought them back to me, they were white as a ghost.   Looked like they were drugged or something. No. Not drugged, it looked like they had their blood sucked out of them.

JW: Some may have been alive, I don't know; don't care really.   But my part of the deal was always the same – "Off with their heads Jimbo," Walt would say and I gave them the axe.

JW: I called the house on North Coat the chopping block.   [laughs]   Yeah, the old fucking chopping block, it was. Shit, we must have chopped off at least a dozen heads before we burnt the place down. That wasn't the only house we torched on the street, but we had to make it look good.

JW: They did good – Old man Walt and TC. We had a real operation going. I made a thousand a head, but any cops listening to this don't try finding it because I spent it.

JW: Okay.

[sigh]

JW: So after about the eleventh or twelfth person, we had to burn down the chopping block house. I thought the operation was over. Then about two weeks later, TC shows up with an unconscious girl and leaves her on my back porch.

JW: I asked TC what the fuck he thought he was doing and he said just deal with it the way I did the others.   I'm like, yea, sure.   Remember, we burnt down the houses!

JW: TC shrugged his shoulders and left. That's what he did, he fucking left. And he left the girl on my back porch.

JW: What he and Walt were expecting me to do was another head chop and mine dump. What I did was just the mine dump.

JW: He brought about thirteen more men and women over the month and it was becoming so obvious I was sure someone would catch on.   There were just too many of them.

JW: Anyway, after the arsons, that was the last decapitation. All the rest of the bodies still have their heads, so if you're up to looking for them, they are in the Runners Ridge Mine, about a fifteen minute walk into the left secondary shaft. There is one hell of a hole, so watch out or you will join them at the bottom.

JW: One day in the middle of all this, Walt asked what I was doing with the heads, as he wanted them. I told you he was a sick old fuck. I told him I threw them in the mine shaft with their bodies. I don't have a clue what he needed them for and didn't ask. He still paid me my cut, so I didn't ponder it.

JW: I thought I could handle it; I really did. That was until I heard noises coming up from deep within the mine. They were groans – groans of the undead!

JW: That was on the twentieth or so trip. At first, I thought it was the drugs I was on. Believe me, you have to be high to do this kind of shit. However, I was stone cold sober the next visit and I heard them again.

JW: Now, I hear them every time I go to bed. That's why I stopped going in to the mine. That Shirley chick I left just as you go through the fence near the mine entrance. That girl Mary is still at my house. She'll be found soon and I'll be dead.

JW: But, anyway, that's the deal and everything I have told you is true. And you can believe me or not, I really don't give a fuck. But, all I know is vampires are real, Walt is dead, and TC is crazy. Watch out for him. There, I've said it and spoke my peace. So, whatever happens will happen.

[click]

CHAPTER 3

On a hill near the edge of town and just beyond the college, lies Jacobs Cemetery.

When Melas was a town, this was where the townsfolk came to bury their dead.

After the brutal murder of Mitch Ryan and the disappearance of the body of young Ralph Edwards – the cemetery's last internment – no one else would go there, claiming it was haunted.

On more than one occasion, people would claim that on certain nights, a ghastly apparition of a young boy could be seen walking amongst the hills. Those who live to tell such a tale all describe the boy as being around nine years old with sandy hair and matches the description of Ralph "Ralphie" Edwards to a tee.

Four members of the Edwards family lost their lives on that fateful night, but only one body was found; that of little Ralphie.

In fact Ralphie and his younger brother Timmy were attacked by a creature of darkness. His older brother Mike and his dad Martin went searching for them; neither returned.

Ralphie made it home just in time to let his family know they were attacked. Ralphie himself had lost a lot of blood and his mother Cathy had taken the young boy to the hospital. A few hours later, he died.

The last thing nine-year-old Ralphie Edwards remembered that night was a feeling that he was about to throw-up. The hospital room was spinning so fast, he thought he was going to be thrown from the bed.

He had to get out of this place. His heart was racing and he felt so cold. "I am freezing!" he thought, "I must get out of here."

His mother, Cathy Edwards, had just left the room to get something to drink. "Mom, don't leave!" he wanted to scream, but he was too weak to even look up at her.

When she left, he tried to get up and go after her, however the very act of getting off the bed proved too much for him.

With a hard crash, he fell to the cold green tiled floor of Unity Hospital and slipped into death's black slumber.

When he opened his eyes, he was trapped in cold darkness. He was in some kind of box. "Help!" he cried, but there was no reply.

He tried to get up, but hit his head on the box's ceiling. The walls and ceiling were satin. "Where am I?" he thought. His panic-stricken mind raced.

He clawed at the box top, ripping some of the fabric. A dull fear settled over him as he realized he was in a casket.

"Oh, no!" Ralphie screamed. "I'm being buried alive!" He pounded again, but to no avail. After a while, he closed his eyes and waited.

26

Many hours later, Ralphie could hear the sound of rolling thunder. A storm was coming. With each rumble, he found himself getting eager to escape. He also realized he was incredibly hungry, wait, not so much hungry, but thirsty. "Yes," Ralphie thought, "I am thirsty... so very thirsty."

At some point, the overwhelming sensation of thirst became so unbearable that Ralphie cried. His eyes stung as he lay in the darkness of the casket.

With every effort he could muster, he struck the top of the box with both hands and to his astonishment, the lid sprung open.

Instantly, he was drenched in hard rain. He looked around and found he was lying in a grave, but the grave had not been closed. Mud and rainwater were pouring into the casket as he lay there.

"Ugh!" Ralphie said to himself and got to his feet. He jumped from the casket and found he actually went several feet into the air, enough to free him from the confines of the grave. "Wow!" he thought to himself, "I have never jumped that high before!"

Standing next to the grave was a man, probably the caretaker and person who was burying him alive. Ralphie thought he might recognize him from somewhere, maybe church, but could not be sure.

One thing he did notice was that even in the pouring rain, he could see the man's pulse. He could see blood pumping through the man and at the sight of this perceived blood Ralphie's thirst grew even more. It had to be satisfied.

Ralphie didn't think; he leapt onto the man and thrust his mouth into the man's neck. Warm blood mixed with rain water poured into Ralphie's mouth and down his throat. He felt so alive.

Somewhere in the distance, like a vague memory, he could hear the man scream.

***

Ralphie Edwards felt as if he were living in a nightmare that he could never wake up from. He had never been to Jacobs Cemetery before and it took him all night to find his way home.

Once he got there, he found the place to be empty. In his clouded mind, he could vaguely remember that fateful night in the woods only a few days earlier. Perhaps he would remember it more, perhaps he would forget it.

He remembered that his brother Timmy and he were going fishing over at Floyd Lake. It was dark and they had taken a shortcut behind the Methodist Church. It had gotten very dark, very quickly. Ralphie and Timmy were so scared.

Then that *thing* attacked them. It grabbed Timmy and dragged him off into the darkness beyond. Then it came for him. Ralphie fought to escape the thing's clutches the best that a nine-year-old boy could, he even bit the monster hard enough to draw blood.

"Aah, blood!" Ralphie thought, his mind temporarily distracted from the recollection at the thought of blood. "The monster's blood was cold and the taste - rancid," Ralphie remembered.

He remembered the creature biting him in the neck just as he bit the creature in the wrist that held him. The creature muttered something and left him alone in the dark.

Ralphie found his way home that night, and his mother Cathy rushed him to the hospital. That was all he could remember.

Once again, he was at his house and, once again, it was night. This time, neither his mother nor father could not be found. His older brother Mike could not be found either.

For the entire night, Ralphie set alone on the living room couch and cried. As he sobbed, he wiped tears of blood from his face. When the first rays of sunlight streamed through the windows, Ralphie felt a burning sensation that he had never felt before. It was as if his skin was on fire. He screamed and ran into his basement to hide.

Light was still streaming through a window well and Ralphie fled toward a utility door leading into a crawlspace deep under the house. Ralphie feared dark, enclosed spaces, but the light was unbearable. Shrieking, he dove into the crawlspace and slammed the utility door shut.

***

Cathy Edwards, Ralphie's mother had spent the night with her sister Mary because she was wrecked with grief and inconsolable.

She attended her son's funeral alone. He husband, Martin, and her other two sons, Mike and Timmy, went missing and were unaccounted for. The police had started to question Cathy as a prime suspect in their disappearances.

"I have to take a walk," Cathy told Mary on the morning after the funeral.

"Sure," Mary replied. "I understand."

Cathy walked down the lonely streets of Melas, mumbling to herself. She was lost within her grief and every fiber of her being knew that her husband and other sons were dead – just like Ralphie.

She wept and moaned. Stumbling out onto the street, she didn't see Pastor Holland driving a church van loaded with "Meals on Wheels" – food for hungry people in the area who could not get out to buy groceries due to age or health.

The pastor recently had a considerably large meat donation from Melas City Councilman Glen Thomas and the baked steak dinners were on the menu today. One of the trays in the front seat shifted and Pastor Holland took his eyes off the road for a split second as he reached for the plate. At that very moment, Cathy Edwards stepped out in front of him and he slammed into her with the church van.

She flipped up onto the front windshield and shattered the glass.

"Good heavens!" Pastor Holland screamed and he slammed on the brakes. Food trays throughout the van flew to the floor.

The pastor got out of the van and ran over to the woman who lay bleeding in the road. He recognized her as a church member and had preached at her son's funeral service just a day before.

"Cathy!" he yelled. The lady on the pavement did not move but was breathing.

Forty-five minutes later, an ambulance arrived and took Cathy Edwards to Unity Hospital for medical treatment. Witnesses who saw the accident said that she was talking to herself and stepped in front of the vehicle without looking.

Arrangements were made to have her sent to the Weston State Lunatic Asylum for psychiatric evaluation after she recovered from her immediate injuries.

Glen Thomas, who heard about the accident, hurried out to the scene to help Pastor Holland get the meals out since the pastor's van was wrecked. It was the least he could do.

***

As the ambulance rolled away hauling Cathy Edwards off for an indefinite stay in the State's care, Ralphie lay death-like in the crawlspace underneath his house.

This was when the dreams began.

They all started the same way. Ralphie was in the woods with his brother Timmy on the night they were killed. Fishing poles in hand, they were wondering aimlessly in a dense forest trying to get somewhere. "Where are we going?" Ralphie would think to himself.

That fateful evening, the two young boys were going catfishing at Floyd Lake. Ralphie and Timmy had taken a shortcut through the woods and had gotten lost.

Victor Rothenstein was hungry and on the hunt. He had killed Timmy, the younger of the boys, first and almost killed Ralphie when he became distracted and left on other matters, but not until he had fed from Ralphie. Ralphie had struggled and bit Victor on the hand hard enough to draw blood.

That was the real event. The dream was slightly different.

Ralphie was in the woods like before and it was night. This time, instead of absolute darkness of the deep wood, the forest was cast in a dense fog.

Although it was still night, Ralphie could see his way clearly.

When his dreams first began, he was simply running through the woods, fleeing from Victor Rothenstein. Just as the vampire caught him, Ralphie would wake up and it would be night.

***

32

Ralphie's heart was racing and he screamed in the dark crawlspace, unsure where he was. The dream was so REAL, so VIVID. Ralphie shook with terror, thinking that if he simply turned his head on the dirt floor in which he lay, he would see Victor's undead face, fangs extended, ready to eat him alive. Or worse yet, maybe he would see Timmy, throat slit and blood drained from his lifeless body.

Ralphie screamed, but he was only answered with silence. Tears of blood streamed down his eyes. He did not realize this. It was only until twenty minutes or so had passed that he remembered where he was — lying in a crawlspace – and made his way back into the basement of his house.

As he stepped out of the crawlspace, he bumped his head on the small door frame that separated the crawlspace from the rest of the basement. *Funny, that should have hurt*, he thought to himself. It was then that Ralphie noticed that he no longer had feeling in his skin. He punched the cinderblock wall and looked at his knuckles. Tiny droplets of blood came to the surface where his skin had been scuffed – still no sensation. "What's happening to me?" he yelled.

Half-panicked, he realized that he had lost feeling in his fingers, though he was still able to move them. Although he lost physical *feeling*, he still felt *emotions*. This was very strange for the young boy.

He climbed up the stairs to the kitchen. With each step, a growing dread took hold and he *knew*, just knew that the house would be empty.

"Mom, Dad?" Ralphie cried out. There was no reply.

"Mike? Timmy?" Still no answer.

Ralphie made it to the living room and turned on the television. The local news came on.

The anchor – Dirk McCallahan – was talking about the top news story:

"Authorities today discovered the body of Mitch Ryan brutally murdered near a dug up grave at Jacobs Cemetery in Melas. There is speculation that he might have caught a grave robbery in progress and the perpetrator retaliated."

The camera cut away to the image of a man with a suit. The words "Detective Mathue" appeared under him.

"Whoever did this is a real sicko and extremely dangerous. We are still investigating the incident, but it appears that Mr. Ryan's throat was bitten out of his neck.

"The grave was also robbed and the body was taken." The detective shook his head in disgust.

Drik McCallahan's image came back on, "The body was that of nine-year-old Melas resident Ralph Edwards…"

As the news trailed off Ralphie screamed, "I'm not dead! I'm right here!"

He left the television on and ran out into the night.

CHAPTER 4

Bobby Luellan stood by the side of the road contemplating lunch. Someone had struck a deer with their car and the carcass of the dead animal lay on the side of the road.

Bobby couldn't be certain if the deer had been killed yesterday or the day before, the only thing he knew was that he was hungry and some fresh deer meat sounded pretty good. He also viewed himself as a thrifty sort of fellow and if he didn't have to buy groceries, that meant more of the disability check he could keep.

He pulled out a large, lock-blade, Buck-branded hunting knife and proceeded to gut the deer there on the roadside. Several cars passed and slowed down to inspect what Bobby was doing. None of them actually stopped, however.

Bobby whistled as he worked and once he was satisfied that one of the deer's hind quarters had been successfully removed from its main body, he cleaned his knife and put it away.

By this point, Bobby was salivating profusely and spittle was running down his chin. Grinning from ear to ear, he raised the newly prepared hind quarter to his lips and began eating it. The raw deer meat never tasted so good!

"What the fuck?" yelled a passing motorist from his rolled-down window. "Get out of the street you nut!"

Bobby paid no mind but continued to eat his meal oblivious to any health consequences or public opinion that some 'passerby' might have.

Once he had consumed the entire hind quarter, Bobby realized that he was no longer hungry. He also forgot about taking the rest of the deer carcass home.

He simply turned from the body and began walking the three-mile path back to a little trailer that he shared with his mother in Wolf Summit.

***

Around the same time that night as Bobby was heading home, Ralphie was making his way through the deserted streets of Melas.

The headlines in the newspaper told how the region was in shock after the discovery of the town's candy maker Diane Dickland and her husband were found brutally murdered in their little downtown confectionary. Ralphie was there. In fact, it was he who killed Diane, but he vaguely remembered it. To Ralphie, it was all like a dream.

Even this evening was strange and dream-like. Ralphie felt as if he were walking through a cloudy mist, making his way through the town and steadily along Raccoon Run Road. The road wound up a tall hill to the old Madison House perched at its top. Tonight, he was not going to the Madison House but toward a faint green glow in the distance. He was not sure why he was heading towards the glow, only that he felt sure he would find answers once he found the source of its light.

After walking steadily uphill for about a half hour, Ralphie stood before a ten-foot tall obelisk. It was the source of the light he was following.

The obelisk pulsed from a bright green to a softer green then repeated. Ralphie sat at the base of the structure and within minutes became hypnotized by the pulsing light.

Some unknown amount of time passed as Ralphie stared unblinking at the glow. Eventually Ralphie dozed off and began dreaming for real.

He was standing in a large field and a very tall winged demon stood before him. The creature had talons for hands and when it opened its mouth, it revealed razor sharp incisors.

Ralphie was scared but did not try to flee.

"Do you know why you are here?" The creature asked.

"No," Ralphie replied. "Where am I?"

"You are in the land of the undead," the creature replied. "I have summoned you."

"Why?" Ralphie asked. That was all he could get out of his mouth.

"I once walked the earth but am now trapped here. You can free my spirit. If you will help me, I will give you your heart's desire.

Ralphie's mind was filled with visions of his past life, his friends, his brothers and his parents. All but his mother were faded, ghost-like creatures that scared Ralphie more than comforted him. His mother, however, looked alive and lost. He saw her looking all over for him. "Mom," he cried out, "I'm right here!" but she did not hear him.

Ralphie wanted his mom very badly. He wanted this nightmare to end.

As if sensing his distress, the demon proclaimed, "You must now make a choice."

The creature bent down to eye level with the boy vampire. "You must choose now to serve me or you will die the true death and join the lost for eternity."

Ralphie was frightened. Although he was technically dead, or more accurately *undead*, he did not know it. For the little boy, Ralphie still thought he was alive. All he knew was that he feared this creature and didn't want to die.

Tears of blood streamed down Ralphie's face. "I do not want to die," Ralphie said. "I just want to see my mother."

"I will take you to your mother," the creature replied. "All in due time."

"Now, I require an answer, boy!" demanded the creature. "Will you serve me?"

"Yes," Ralphie replied. His panic was suddenly replaced by relief and a wave of pleasurable happiness washed over him. "Who are you?"

"You can call me Master."

***

In the weeks and months that followed, Ralphie would make nightly pilgrimages to the obelisk to commune with the demon. In this time, he grew supernaturally wiser – much more than his years – in the ways of the vampire.

During this time, he lived off the blood of various farm animals in the surrounding areas. Although he vaguely remembered that he enjoyed human blood after drinking from Diane Dickland that first night in her candy shop, the sensation and worry that fell on his conscious afterwards was almost too much for the nine-year-old to bear. He did not have the same reservations with the farm animals that surrounded the small town.

One night, a mysterious visitor approached Ralphie as he was deep in trance. This person wore a cloak that resembled the attire that a druid or warlock might wear.

Ralphie's keen ears heard the man approach. He spun around, revealing his razor-sharp incisors.

"Be calm little one," the man said in a commanding tone. "I am not here to harm you."

Ralphie hissed, not completely convinced of the man's sincerity. "Who dares to disturb us?" Ralphie asked in a commanding voice that was not his own. Ralphie realized that it was the demon speaking through him.

"It is I, Talman," the cloaked man announced. "Is that you Legion?"

"You buffoon!" the demonic voice roared through Ralphie. "I am back on the *other* side. Do you hear me? It took centuries to get out of hell and now I am back in hell!"

"Legion, I had no idea," Talman replied awkwardly.

"That's right. You had no idea," Legion replied angrily. Ralphie's eyes glowed with rage. The small boy was briefly transformed into the avatar of the large winged beast. It reached out and grabbed the man by the throat, lifting him off the ground with one talon-like hand. "I would kill you right where you stand if you were not of our master's own flesh."

"It is neither I nor my brother that has betrayed you. Through the centuries, we have always done our father's bidding."

The demon sat Talman back on the ground, its anger temporarily abated. "But surely, you must have some explanation as to how things got so fucked up?" The demon spread its wings at the same time making an open arm gesture. "By all means, please explain."

"Where do I start?" asked Talman. "I myself do not know how Victor got killed or even how you disappeared."

40

He stepped forward, looking the demon straight into his eyes. "Victor and Walt *assured* us that sending you to America would allow you to manifest in true flesh, not just spirit. Henry and I personally performed the sanguinary rituals *exactly* as father described.

"In fact, Henry loaded the railroad box personally with your essence in Berlin. The Nazis had hidden it for decades after the war.

"And I sent this very obelisk to Victor clear back in the 1930s from Transylvania." Talman pointed at the glowing green stone. "He and Walter worked for years to get the gateway to Hell opened. It should have been easy for you to physically manifest once your remains were near it here in West Virginia. Tell me Legion, were you successful?"

"Momentarily, it would seem." Legion replied. "Victor told me that when I arose from eternal sleep, I would be fed a feast of living souls; to drink deeply from their blood and come into my full powers. I would be the dragon servant to our master.

"When the box was opened, there was only one living person to feed on." Legion's eyes grew crimson red with a chaotic glow, "*It* didn't even come close to quenching my thirst."

The demon began pacing in circles around Talman. "Victor had me in some kind of pit below his domicile."

"The basement cellar?" Talman mused.

"There was no blood there," Legion replied. "So I went on a hunt that night and found where he put my prey."

"Which was where?" Talman asked.

"A large fort near his domicile; I flew there that night and feed on a multitude of souls. Many were children like my young protégée here."

For a moment, Talman thought Legion was describing Fort Melas, a nearby historical site not too far off the main highway. But that couldn't be, as Victor always kept a low profile. He wouldn't have risked a possible car passing by and taking notice of a ten-foot-wide bat flying overhead. This didn't make sense.

Then it hit him, there was only one place that had so many children that would be open at night: the Melas Industrial Home For Troubled Youth. "Jesus Christ, I can't believe it. You attacked the school!"

Legion punched Talman so hard it sent him flying over twenty feet and outside the immediate glow of the obelisk. He pinned him down on the ground, bearing his full mouth of razor-sharp teeth. "Don't you ever say that name around me!"

Talman was stunned and momentarily forgot the comment that brought the demon's wrath. Suddenly he remembered and began laughing profusely on the cold ground. "I almost forgot, you two go way back! Sorry to bring up a sore spot. I can see why dad likes you so much."

Legion growled at him and stood up.

Legion continued his retrospective, "The fort, or school as you say, was a trap. I killed many that night and with each life, I drank blood and grew stronger. Then a great fire overtook me and my very essence was incinerated. My soul was sent back into Hell once again!"

"It looks like you have some misdirected anger, Legion," Talman replied, this time standing up himself.

He straightened out his cloak and continued, "Victor didn't set you up. You attacked a school. The place exploded that very night. I always wondered what happened. You must have set the place on fire with you being all demonic and shit."

"I did NOT burn it down!" Legion screamed. "Do you think me to be a fool, Talman?"

"Not at all, Legion," Talman replied. "But something caught the Industrial Home on fire that night and I know it wasn't Victor. And it wasn't Walter or Jimbo either, as those two were dead when it happened."

Legion growled. "Where were you and your cambion brother that night?"

"Just chill out," Talman said. "Father had us renew our contract with him. We've been just a few miles downstream in Tarklin. I got me a job at the funeral home and Henry is working at the insane asylum in Weston. When he's not there, he's on Tarklin's water board." Talman grinned something sinister and added, "We could use your help."

"It takes years to manifest in my true form," Legion replied.

"Maybe," Talman added. "But you do have a vessel before you in the boy." Choosing his words carefully, he added, "He would make a nice... possession."

CHAPTER 5

Talman Cane needed some*body*. This time, he would be particular about which body he chose, since it would become his own.

Talman Cane had worked with a certain James Whilder, luring innocents to bring as victims for vampire Victor Rothenstein. They had worked quiet quietly and successfully sourcing blood donors for their Master, but Whilder had ruined it all now. Upon the release of Jimbo Whilder's confessional tape to the police, implicating Talman as an accessory to serial killing, he had found it necessary to change his identity, once again. Unlike those humans who do not make a contract with the devil in return for eternal life, for the Cane brothers, this involved more than a new name, dark glasses, false papers and extra facial hair. It was an altogether greater and all-encompassing affair. This was one of the advantages of immortality and a contract with Satan – their Father – gave them both the ability to shapeshift and to change bodies whenever the need arose – and especially when in danger of discovery.

Still, the need existed for Talman Crane's dark works to continue in the service of Victor Rothenstein, and mere physicality would not hold him back from this grim purpose. His brother Henry Cane, with an established reputation as a pillar of the community and a respectable job as a doctor, was still able to continue his evil work in the Weston State Lunatic Asylum undisturbed. But this time, Talman Cane – fingered as a serial killer - was obliged to seek out another host body.

"Your carelessness has provoked this action, Talman," Henry Cane said through gritted teeth, glaring at his brother through his steel-rimmed spectacles, his face otherwise impassive, "I trust your idiocy will not manifest itself again this century. The least you can do this time is to select a body with a brain - one that actually works."

Used to his brother's scything sarcasm, Talman said nothing in his defense. After all, since he had his choice of host body, Henry was right: he might as well select one that would serve all purposes. Envious of Henry's lifestyle and intelligence, Talman made a decision to choose wisely this time, and well.

And so, Talman Cane had moved from Melas to nearby Tarklin, and marked out a certain Josef McClumpy as his target. He had a healthy, attractive young body, with many years of use ahead of it, but enough smarts, maturity and standing to guarantee that Talman could use the whole package to his advantage in the community. And, he had a very compelling line in business that fitted well with Talman's dark purpose. There were only a couple of tasks ahead that Talman needed to complete, and then he could slip easily into a respectable role himself – as Josef McClumpy.

This innocent man of twenty-nine was unaware of his terrible fate, even when his way was barred on the curb by a strange cloaked man. Josef smiled easily, and went to side-step around Talman's figure, in the way that a normal person does, when accidentally stepping into someone else's path. He even said, "Sorry!"

Then the dark man stepped sideways in the same direction, barring Josef's way again.

Josef laughed, in the same way a normal person does when two people misunderstand each other's intentions, and step in one another's way, instead stepping around one another.

"Ha! Sorry again!" Josef grinned, tickled by the farcical dance they were doing. He looked up into the man's face, expecting to see a similar grin or at least a polite smile in return. But as he glanced up, his own smile froze.

Josef was unaware of his fate even while he stared into the stranger's intense eyes in the street, and the snarling expression which locked him in a fearsome paralysis; until he felt his very soul torn out of his chest and wisp away from him like smoke. Bewildered, from a position a few feet in the air above the scene, Josef watched his own body, still unaccountably standing, then walking and still living, and could not believe what he saw. Nor did he understand what had happened to him until his soul was violently sucked down into Hell and faced Satan himself, in all his fiery glory.

All was red-hot and consumed by fire. Satan's huge, all-encompassing and flaming face rose from the depths, blood-red eyes staring with wicked sparks of amusement, lurid red and gold fiery tongues licking and spitting from his horned head. He inhaled the soul of the real Josef McClumpy and he laughed heartily, shaking his head so that red-hot cinders and ash sprayed around.

"Ha ha! Keep them coming, my sons! There is not enough evil in the world to feed my voracious hunger for souls!" he roared. "One at a time is like feeding a single potato chip into the Grand Canyon. You cannot expect me to be satisfied with such meager fare! What we need is another world war, boys! I enjoyed the last one you gave me!" He laughed cruelly, the laughter echoing around and reverberating until it disappeared with him to the depths of Hell, from whence he came.

That was the end of the real Josef McClumpy's life, and his soul, yet his body continued on. The only difference was that his body was now controlled and assumed by the old Talman Cane – who was fully embodied as Josef McClumpy and ready to take on his life, his work… and his family.

Josef McClumpy's father owned the McClumpy Funeral Home in Tarklin. It was a large, rambling family home and business. Neo-gothic in style, with dark arched windows and tiled roof spires on the two round stone towers which framed the whole building, the vision of it suited its funereal purpose. It looked like a place of the dead, even though the funeral business itself was confined to the basement. It was the stereotypical haunted house. Local kids for generations had dared one another to go near it, referencing Frankenstein, The Addams Family and The Munsters. Consequently, the latest McClumpys, sick and tired of young daredevils and kids knocking on doors to run away or peering through windows, had invested in a sophisticated security system, which started at the tall electric gates to the driveway, and ended at the CCTV cameras outside the house and state-of-the art iris recognition and fingerprint identification technology within the building itself. Later generations would call it Fort Knox, because it was impossible for anyone to enter without invitation or appointments.

Strangely, within a day of Talman appearing on the scene within his son's body, old Lawrence McClumpy died suddenly of mysterious circumstances. It was a horrifying and shocking discovery for poor Josef the next morning, after he called the police for help, like the good citizen he was. Strangely, his father was missing from the main house, and when attempting to enter the business premises, poor Josef had been unable to gain access to the basement room, despite de-activating the sophisticated alarm system. This was most disturbing and irregular. Josef called the police, immediately suspicious, and a patrol car had arrived within a few minutes. The McClumpys were politically powerful people, and Lawrence was a personal friend and golfing buddy of the Sheriff. When the McClumpys wanted something, the authorities jumped to attend to their wishes.

It took the police less than ten minutes to batter down the door, upon Josef's request. The scene before them was one that the two attending police officers would never forget. There, was the pajama-clad body of Lawrence, waxen and dead, in his own basement embalming room. Worse, Lawrence McClumpy appeared to have slowly drained out his own blood, binding his biceps with a constricting broad elasticated band, crudely cutting a vein in his wrist and allowing his blood to flow down the drain in the trough. Horrifically still, then he attended to his other arm with a needle, attaching it to the tube of his pumping machine, and with the last of his strength, his final act was to only just begin the process of pumping the vein of his other arm full of embalming fluid, leaving it to complete the job after he died. By the time poor Josef and the police had discovered him, the machine was still whirring away doing its job, as instructed, and old McClumpy was almost completely embalmed.

Or 'dill-pickled', as the new Josef – Talman Cane – snickered to himself.

The local press had a field day, and even The National Enquirer, television stations, and other news services reported the bizarre affair. It was the oddest suicide the state police and coroner had ever come across, yet the room had been found locked and bolted from the inside, and no signs of force, or strangers' fingerprints had been found. Only the phrase 'Goodbye cruel world,' scrawled on a nearby blood-stained notepad, was Lawrence McClumpy's only indication of his solitary intent.

The locals speculated, and made up all manner of ludicrous stories about Lawrence McClumpy's presumed business failure, depression, money troubles, even homosexuality - but nobody knew the real reason

51

for the suicide. There was no obvious reason for Lawrence to end his life: the business had been thriving. As he was wont to joke with close friends and family: "There's nothing like death to make you a good living."

The reality was that Talman had simply called up his employer, Victor Rothenstein, and invited him over to dinner on an evening when he knew his dad would be home late.

Since the outdoor CCTV cameras were only attuned to ground-level threats, they did not pick up on the presence of a large bat flying through the sky.

Talman had easily offered his Master entrance to the house via an upstairs attic window out of the cameras' field of view, and led him swiftly through the domain to the downstairs embalming room, discussing his proposal in urgent whispers.

Once Victor was in place and the trap perfectly set, Josef headed back upstairs to wait on his father's return from the evening's social affair.

"Dad!" Josef yelled, as his father stepped out of his car. "Come and see my new idea to finesse the embalming process!"

Lawrence looked askance at his son, "At this time, Joe? Can't it wait?"

But looking at his son's honest blue eyes, full of enthusiasm and pride, he relented, and laughed,

"Okay, son. Never one to stand in the way of progress; let's see what you've got for us!"

He got more than he bargained for.

Once down in the basement, Victor Rothenstein stepped immediately forward and old McClumpy was mesmerized by his compellingly intent and hypnotic stare, and found himself completely paralyzed. Although unable to move a muscle, he remained horribly conscious and aware of everything that occurred thereafter, throughout the whole painful and lengthy process of having every drop of blood sucked out of him by a real vampire.

Whilst Victor preferred to drink fresh, hot blood straight from the throat, where the gush from the jugular vein or carotid artery was greater in force and more satisfying, he resentfully consented to sink his teeth into the vein of the old man's wrist, and suck headily from there.

"There's no way anyone would be convinced that he had the time to drain his own blood AND fit the tube to the embalming pump and start it - while his jugular was gushing..." explained Talman, with all the professional knowledge of Josef McClumpy at his disposal.

Rothenstein salivated at the thought of arterial spray and gushing veins, "Surely he could have strapped himself up to the embalming fluid pumping machine and THEN severed his jugular?" he snarled in disbelief, suspicious of being cheated or taken for a fool by Talman Cane.

Lawrence McClumpy, completely immobilized, could only stare, wildly, in terror and disbelief. This would be a lengthy process. His hearing was fine. His mind worked too well. His body, unfortunately, experienced all the painful cuts and ferocious, stinging sucks of the vampire, desperate for his blood. If only these bodily functions and sensations had been completely removed too, along with his ability to move. He could not even will himself to black out.

"You wouldn't want the blood contaminated by embalming fluid for your drinking..." explained Talman, "Ordinarily, we make small incisions in both vessels, so the tube connected to the embalming fluid pump goes in the carotid artery, and the drain tube goes in the jugular vein. We pump embalming fluid through the artery, and this makes the blood come back through the veins and flow out into the drain. There's usually only one point of injection of the embalming fluid, except when clots stop the flow ..."

"Shut up, Cane! I am doing this purely for the amusement factor," grimaced Rothenstein, lifting his bloody mouth from the arm, where he had been sucking so furiously that he was light-headed and dizzy, "I am entertained by the particular context of an embalming room and willing to play along with the ridiculous circumstances I find myself in, and the intriguing set-up you propose, simply to safeguard your new role here... Even though this is like trying to suck gravy through a child's drinking straw. Do not think that I will consent to this arrangement on another occasion. It fits well tonight, and it mildly amuses me. But in future, I want copious amounts of fresh blood on MY terms!"

Talman bowed graciously, marveling at the flexibility of Josef McClumpy's fit body, and how well he wore it himself.

As the only surviving son, Josef just happened to inherit the Funeral Home, so since Talman Cane had fortuitously stepped in, he easily assumed that responsibility too, and planned to run the business as a respectable man, becoming a pillar of the community - just like his own brother, Doctor Henry Cane, at the Weston State Lunatic Asylum.

Josef McClumpy's body had given him a great start in this small community – the man had already been generally well-liked in the town, and his family was one of the old guard. Highly respected for generations, the McClumpys were known to everyone, and there was hardly an individual that they weren't related to in some way, or hadn't buried...

Besides, thought the new Josef McClumpy/old Talman Cane, *You never know when you're going to need a good undertaker in this business.*

To the good folks of Tarklin, out and about in the community, he was simply amiable Josef McClumpy: smartly but modestly suited; employing a modest and loyal group of employees; sympathizing graciously with the recently bereaved; handling delicate affairs with integrity and decorum; smiling appropriately; drinking socially but moderately with the guys; never cussing, always civil; raising his hat politely at ladies; attending church on Sundays. He was the very model of gentility and a true and generous citizen.

Inside, though, he was still Talman Cane, evil to the very core.

Although perhaps not as evil as his brother, Doctor Henry Cane, and his experiments at the Asylum…

***

Weston State Lunatic Asylum was a hospital built in 1858, and was a huge place: the largest hand-cut stone masonry building in the whole of North America. It had long rambling wings and wards, staggered in a V-shape to allow the circulation of fresh air and sunlight, in an attempt to cure the 'lunatics.'

The original hospital was designed to accommodate two hundred and fifty souls, but reached its climax in the 1950s with 2,400 patients living in terrible, overcrowded, and poor conditions.

Whilst not reaching anything like those numbers, the present hospital was full to overcrowding. Large areas of the hospital building had deteriorated, and half of the wards were left abandoned, locked off and secured, while any available money went into the upkeep of the remaining wing, where 300 mentally ill people were cramped into space designed to house one hundred and twenty five.

This was by no means the worst treatment of mentally ill people. Early colonists in North America believed that people with mental illness were possessed by demons, witches, or even by the Devil himself. Recent psychological studies of the documents from the Salem Witch Trials in 1692, telling of the symptoms displayed by those accused, suggest that most of the executed "witches" were more likely insane.

"But not all," smiled Henry Cane to himself. His and Talman's mother had been a witch in Salem at the time, and was surely not mentally ill. She knew exactly what she was doing when she had communed with the Devil for real, and ridden laughingly and whoreishly on his broomstick. Her sons, Henry and Talman were the living proof of that.

Henry could not help but smile at the irony of the fact that he was now the Doctor treating the psychiatric patients in the hospital. When once in days of witch-hunting, the fear had been that these mentally ill souls were possessed by demonic forces which manifested themselves in the symptoms of schizophrenia, bi-polar disorder, depression, paranoia, hysteria, personality disorders and other mental health problems – now, it was Henry Cane's evil purpose to ensure that such patients WERE possessed by demons, witches and his father – the Devil himself.

He found it hilarious, this switch-around, and often laughed within himself. However, his external persona was not the sort to show his emotional state. He was not so generous as to give anything of himself to another. Least of all to a human. And only because he and his brother were under contract with their father the Devil to supply him with souls for his evil dominion, and since their father gifted both of his sons with immortality on condition that they pursued lives of wickedness, it was only for the selfishness of eternal life that he did anything for his father at all.

And after all, Henry Cane smirked, the patients these days were not badly treated. He himself had lived through the good old days of the 1700s, when even by his standards, the treatment for mentally ill people was quite barbaric. Unless their family cared for them, they were put in prisons with common criminals, chained to walls, unclothed, and left in their own shit and piss. Other mad people, kept at home, were locked in attics or sheds and holes in the ground. What a thrill his doctoring would have been then, with no regulations or authorities, and no one that cared. Only in the 1770's were buildings built especially to house the insane. But these were to keep the individual away from society, and insanity was believed to be incurable.

In the 1800's the plight of the insane was brought to the attention of the public, who called for more humane levels of care. By mid-century, the theory of creating a curative environment took hold, and the age of the Asylum arrived. Patients moved from being chained naked in cold dark cells in overcrowded city jails and almshouses, to a countryside environment with landscaped grounds, comfortable living quarters and a variety of activities for stimulating patients mentally and physically. Stimulation of a different kind interested Cane.

In the twentieth century, changes in psychiatric treatment, philosophy, and more community based services began, marking the demise of most asylums. The expense of maintaining these large buildings, combined with their gradual deterioration forced many to be abandoned or demolished. Weston still stood proud, however, even into the twenty-first century – based in the remaining wing that was still operational, and was privately funded, with around three hundred patients still receiving care (if what Henry Cane practiced could be called 'care').

His treatments involved a wide range of cruel tortures on the mentally ill, but since no witnesses were present, or permitted to remember what they had experienced, Cane, in his impassive glee, managed to continue his cruel practices undetected.

Henry Came had a unique ability to perform extended acts of torture on his victims through their unconscious mind. To his assistants - and the outside world - he worked normally and ethically. The patients, on the other hand, experienced terrible mental fantasies, where he worked on them in spirit.

He favored young women – or 'patients' as he was now well-used to calling them – as his ideal victims. But he was discriminatory and unequal in his attention, which meant that he was not averse to inflicting the most excruciating pain upon men of all ages, or older women too. They were all as one to him, and he was objective enough not to overindulge his own personal lusts for young women, for he saw such peccadilloes as weakness, and he would never admit to any personal weakness. After all, he was not his brother, Talman.

Henry Cane considered himself to be the brains of the operation, and while both brothers were bound by the intellectual limits of the bodies they took over, Henry had made extremely wise choices in the past. This body and mind he currently used had lasted him for the best part of a century now, and he had so far managed to evade detection throughout all of the worst horrors he had inflicted upon the world.

His brother Talman, in his turn, had chosen the body and intellectual capacity of a low-life idiot last time, in his opinion. Hmm. He would see how he fared this time. Although he boasted that he'd done a great job with his present choice – even comparable to Henry's level in social standing, Henry was doubtful. Talman never thought of the consequences of his actions; never played the long game.

And as Henry wandered the corridors of the Weston State Lunatic Asylum, approaching the reinforced glass of the swing doors, he caught sight of his reflection in them: the high domed forehead with the receding hairline, the acute eyes beyond the inscrutable pebble glasses with wire frames, the unathletic but commanding gait and posture - and he allowed himself a wry smile. No one even recognized him! He was surrounded by idiots. And lunatics.

As he rustled in his pocket for the key to turn in the lock of one cell door, he fixed his smile into one approaching kindness.

After centuries of observing and analyzing human behavior, he knew well how to pass for human. Although he was devoid of any empathy or human emotion beyond anger, pride, lust... He smirked to himself, as a thought occurred to him. He was a walking, talking Seven Deadly Sins. He ran through them in his mind to check: *luxuria* (lechery/lust), *gula* (gluttony), *avaritia* (avarice/greed), *acedia* (acedia/discouragement/sloth), *ira* (wrath), *invidia* (envy), *superbia* (pride). Well, he didn't mind personifying most of those, but perhaps he would defer to Talman with regard to gluttony, sloth and envy.

Re-composing his facial expression to one of benign concern, he slipped the key in the door, and opened it onto the moonlit cell within. There on the bed lay a young man, recently admitted, with porcelain skin and a nervous disposition, Physically, he was strong, and it was interesting to Cane to see how far that physical frame might be pushed, when the limitations of the psyche were stretched.

His first experiments here had been with the physical body, attaching electrodes to various parts of the patients' bodies and observing the results. He was not in the least concerned about patient welfare, cure or progress – but really only interested in the results of the high levels of pain on the body, seeing what happened, how much they could withstand, and observing what effects that had on him, personally.

So, he would attach electrodes to the nipples, clitorises and inside the vaginas of women, and beneath the foreskins, to the scrotum, on the perineum and up the rectums of men, and he would blast them with electricity. He watched their bodies buck and jitter on the beds and tables to which he had strapped them; he saw how much people could withstand; how far he could go without externally burning them and causing suspicious markings which might alert colleagues to malpractice or abuse, and he noticed the thrill he got from each new experiment – with different bodies, different genders, different ages.

He noticed also how the thrill waned and he became acclimatized to the practice. It was never enough for him. To start, there had needed to be more patients, more electrodes, bigger electrical voltage, more sessions, the injection of drugs, the use of no drugs... but none of this satisfied his increasing needs to inflict more pain, to do more evil and to satisfy his intellectual curiosity for scientific experimentation and discovery.

He needed some way to perform the most horrific torture on these incarcerated patients without leaving a single mark on their bodies. And now, he was perfecting that.

He stood, watching a moonbeam cast its pearly silver light over the young man's lower face on the pillow, and a shaft of dark shadow contrasting against its light, obscuring the man's eyes, the windows to the soul. For a moment, Henry simply stood and admired the composition of this picture in his view. In an aesthetic sense, Henry understood that this could be described as a beautiful image. Then he stepped forward, toward the bed.

***

Talman Cane was doing a roaring trade with the McClumpy Funeral Home. He was quite in his element, surrounded by death, reveling in the grief of others. Victor Rothenstein wanted nothing to do with drinking the drained blood of dead people that had already started to clot within their veins, and was cold. However, he was not averse to accepting an offering of home-made blood sausage now and again. Talman thought it was a shame to flush all that valuable human blood down the drain. He hated to see waste.

He browsed the internet and found a recipe, adding his own fine permutations, and asking Rothenstein for his opinions on each different batch. Sometimes he added hot pepper, other spices, occasionally whipping cream. But never garlic. He would stir together a cup of finely chopped onions or shallots and a half a pound of lard, diced or pinched into small gobbets. He added a quarter cup of breadcrumbs, rice or barley, two or three beaten eggs, a pinch of thyme or ground bay leaf and a teaspoon of salt and some pepper. He added all of this into about three cups of human blood – as fresh as he could get it, which was never very fresh. He mixed this mixture well, until the dry ingredients absorbed the blood. If the blood was old and clotted, he occasionally heated the mixture, or added an anticoagulant if he thought Rothenstein wouldn't notice. Otherwise it was the devil of a job to mix it all evenly. He partially filled the sausage casings, to allow for them swelling as they cooked. He boiled a large pan with water alone, or half milk and half water. Then he plunged the sausages into the water and switched the heat down very low for fifteen minutes.

He gave the sausages to Victor Rothenstein, who declared that he preferred them without seasoning and less cooked, but sliced and grilled. Everyone at the Church Potluck Supper liked the ones with cream and herbs, though. Mrs. Winterton begged for the recipe, flirting as hard as her sixty year old heart could, but Talman would only smile and tap his nose mysteriously. He was such a charmer!

He grinned to himself about the nice little sideline he could have here, in a Sweeney Todd the demon barber kind of way. Sweeney Todd made pies from his clients, Talman made delicious blood sausage. No harm done. It's not as if he killed anyone to fulfill customer needs! "Well, maybe that wasn't completely true," he corrected himself.

Although it was surprising just how many husbands, wives, parents and friends of the recently deceased died of broken hearts, poor things. It wasn't just that Talman gave their addresses to Victor Rothenstein, or arranged follow-up home visits. It was a win-win situation. McClumpy's funeral home got a lot more trade, and so did Rothenstein - especially since those bitten needed the heads removed from the corpses to prevent them from joining Victor Rothenstein as vampires. He could do without the competition, frankly. Talman could easily remove the head or dislocate the neck vertebrae as part of the funeral process, and even managed to prepare the corpses for open caskets with aplomb – and a polo-neck, turtle neck, cravat, scarf, or pretty neck corsage with broad velvet choker.

His funeral services were the pride of the town, his blood sausages were a legend, and he was such a lovely, popular, rich, and well-respected man. It wasn't long before that fine gentleman Josef

McClumpy was elected as Mayor of Tarklin. It was nothing less than he deserved!

Talman laughed his own head off, inside.

***

Henry Cane stood over the sleeping young man, who just recently registered and settled into Weston State Lunatic Asylum. His name was Fred Blose. He had been referred by his own doctor, and Henry had not even had the pleasure of assessing him yet.

No matter. Just from an initial glance at him this afternoon carrying his overnight bag through the lobby, and now, lying supine here with one powerful arm out-flung, and his pale but well-toned torso exposed, Henry could see that he was strong of stature, broad shouldered and muscular. But his body language and facial expression on arrival had been timid and self-effacing. Henry found this dichotomy hilarious, yet intriguing. What was going on in there? He couldn't wait to find out and explore the possibilities.

He stared so hard at Fred Blose's face that something in the pressure of the atmosphere alerted Fred to a presence. He woke with a start, seeing the looming dark figure of Henry Cane above him, but unable to recognize him – seeing instead only an imposing black shadow, with moonlight glinting and reflecting off its glassy eyes, like headlamps.

"Wha…?" Fred exclaimed, half asleep and half-rising to sit. But as soon as he caught the fixed stare of Cane, he was lost. He fell back on the bed, unable to control either his body or mind, and Cane was in.

Fred was naked, running through an old, deserted warehouse. He was running for his life. The space was cavernous and dirty. The floors were all stained-grey concrete and walls were marked with old graffiti tags. Litter and a few odd items of discarded metal industrial furniture were strung haphazardly about in no discernable pattern. There was a smell of butchery in the air, as if it was the site of a current abattoir/slaughterhouse, with the tang of metallic blood in the air, and an undercurrent of rotten flesh. All Fred knew was complete terror.

Fred ran, and ran, the sound of his bare feet slapping on the concrete, pounding the ground, running and running, his heart bursting out of his strong chest. Every stride sent him travelling far across the vast space, yet getting nowhere. Still ahead of him there was more vast enclosed concrete space, and still he ran, forever trying to reach a door in the distance, another room, a way out.

He ran, and ran, exhausting himself - feeling himself slowing in pace, and still getting nowhere, until he stopped, doubled over with breathlessness and nausea. He bent down, panting hard, his throat rasping with blood, his pulse throbbing in his ears and his heart still pounding fit to burst through his ribcage.

And so it did – wrenching out of his chest as if ripped by an iron claw! Fred felt it – all the excruciating pain, tearing his skin, flesh and bone - and saw his blood burst out through the cavity it left, splashing onto the floor in front of him in a pool. His heart dangled against his abdomen, still attached by veins and arteries, hanging painfully and beating weakly.

Fred looked down in agony and horror, and did the only thing he could think to do: he took his bleeding and still-beating heart in his hands, where it pumped grotesquely between his fingers, and tried to tuck it back into his chest.

As he held it in with both hands, an ear-piercingly loud, deep laugh filled the warehouse, reverberating off every wall. Fred's own scream joined it. An agonized, heart-rending shriek, using all the pain in his heart and the strength of his lungs – which brought one of the night-staff running to Fred's hospital room to join a concerned Doctor Cane, who had evidently arrived just before her.

"Nightmare," explained Doctor Cane, reassuringly.

The night nurse laughed in relief and left the room to return to her other duties.

Fred muttered something inaudibly and began to scream again, starting with a low whimper and growing louder by the second.

"Now, now, we can't have that!" Dr. Cane said as he looked around the room. He had to find something to fix this. He swiftly walked over to a cabinet and began rummaging through its drawers.

"You don't want to disturb the lovely nurse again, do you, Mr. Blose?"

Fred Blose let out a terrible-sounding wail.

Dr. Cane returned to Fred's bedside, having found just what he was looking for.

"You know how they say, 'Silence is golden?'"

Fred moaned loudly, tears streaking down his face.

"Well, duct tape is silver!"

***

Another thing that tickled Talman Cane about 'Josef McClumpy' – or at least his body being voted Mayor of Tarklin – was that he could now wield a similar power to his brother Henry. Where Henry ruled the madhouse, Talman ruled the mad town, he snickered. Pretty soon, they would be able to do much, much more. Father would be pleased.

And when the time came for a major review of the Tarkiln Water Board, Mayor Josef McClumpy made an excellent recommendation for the professional health expert required to oversee water testing and regulation. Who better than esteemed medical doctor and consultant psychiatrist, Doctor Henry Cane?

CHAPTER 6

In the dead of night at the end of October, on one of Ralphie's regular visits to the obelisk, he sensed the power of Legion surging within him. This was unlike anything he had experienced before. Suddenly from out of the undergrowth, both Talman Cane and – unusually – Henry Cane too stepped forward, to make an unholy trinity.

They stood, cloaked in black, triangulating themselves with Ralphie, and he was aware of deep sensations within him. The gentle green glow of the obelisk grew to a vivid green and a throbbing, pulsating rhythm filled Ralphie's body, mimicking a heartbeat resounding in his chest. And for that time, Ralphie remembered what it was to be human, to be powered by internal organs, yet he knew that any humanity he had left was being controlled – and kept in check by – a far greater external force.

Bubbling up inside him was the urge to speak, although he didn't know what he would say, until he opened his mouth and an ear-blasting sound rang out: "We three are here to complete the Great Plan and to progress the communication of the collective consciousness!" Legion roared.

"It is All Hallows Eve," announced Talman. "The easiest time to commune with the other side. The time when the veil between the worlds is at its thinnest, and the time when spirits walk amongst the living at their ease."

"It is time for the undead to rise!" added Henry Cane, in a commanding voice.

"WAIT!" boomed the voice of Legion, insulted by Henry Cane's imposition.

As Ralphie felt the force of Legion surge within him, he was filled with an all-encompassing knowing and connection. He experienced for the first time a clairvoyant vision of some future time and place known only to his demonic counterpart who he now shared a collective conscious with.

He vividly saw the image of ghouls lying dormant within a cave-like pit. They were in total darkness, but he could see them move – staggering about like shadowy silhouettes in the deep. They were moaning. Suddenly, unimaginable hunger raged through him – he immediately recognized it as the hunger of the collective.

Ralphie momentarily felt an overwhelming power arising within him, filling his small body, vibrating the air around him and surging through the depths of the mine, rushing through every shaft and rivulet of the streams. He felt the force of consciousness, like a torrent of water heavy enough to cut through rock, washing through the mine, and pouring into the dull mind of every ghoul. He felt a spark burst from his mind to the ghouls', like an electric connection: a shock that reanimated them, and brought them within his consciousness. It also was set alight within the knowing of Legion, and that spark zipped around, connecting the minds of every ghoul to one another – and to Legion and Ralphie.

Then the urge to yell overwhelmed him.

"Soon, but NOT YET, will be the time to ARISE!" he cried in the deep booming voice of Legion, its richness and volume making the earth shudder, and the obelisk vibrate with a resonance that filled their ears for minutes afterwards.

And Ralphie knew then, that should there ever be the need to call upon the forces of the undead, he was capable of drawing upon this collective consciousness. In the coming months, that psychic connection would grow, until the time was right. As Legion controlled Ralphie, he had the power now to connect to countless undead bodies, and to work them as one, with his mind. For the moment, he didn't know how or why. He just knew.

CHAPTER 7

Our daily life is not a pleasant one. When we put on our oil soaked suit in the morning we can't guess all the dangers which threaten our lives. We walk sometimes miles to the place- to the man way or traveling way, or to the mouth of the shaft on top of the slope. Add then we enter the darkened chambers of the mines. On our right and on our left we see the logs that keep up the top and support the sides which may crush us into shapeless masses, as they have done to many of our comrades.

-- Article from *The Independent,* circa 1902

DECEMBER 23
TWO YEARS LATER

Pulling onto Dark Hollow Road, Jeff Abraham was filled with mixed emotions. "How in the hell did I go from a desk job to this?" he thought to himself.

He stopped his Lexus LS600 momentarily over the bridge that crossed Bridge Creek and thought about his new job. "Nothing like taking a luxury car to work in the coal mines," he thought.

He looked out over the water. It looked like a large 'river' of rapidly flowing dirt-colored water and ice. Normally, Bridge Creek was nothing more than a tiny stream winding its way from the valley that Dark Hollow was situated in, then onwards around another hill or two, and then over by the town of Melas.

Melas. Now that was another story all together. The town went to hell in a hand basket over the past couple years. Disappearances, murders, mysterious fires – where was it all headed?

Even Jillian got sucked into the madness. Jeff suspected that his wife was cheating on him when she disappeared. In a way, he couldn't really blame her. He was always out working or golfing. If she was lonely and needed a little fun on the side, who was he to deny her? He only wished it hadn't cost her her life. It cost him his career and almost two years in jail over the ordeal, but in a sense, he was the lucky one of the deal.

Bridge Creek seemed larger than usual from this vantage point on the bridge. This winter had been unseasonably cold, but it looked like the spring was starting to thaw things out. Much of the snow had started to melt and that undoubtedly made the water of Bridge Creek rise above its normal levels.

Suddenly, there was a tap on the glass. Jeff gazed out to see an older gentleman, maybe in his fifties. He later learned the man was Kevin Blackthorne, a foreman at the Dark Hollow mine where both men were headed that day.

"Hey buddy, you need some help?" Kevin asked.

Jeff realized he had been idling on the bridge for an undetermined amount of time and was probably holding up traffic. In a way, he was surprised that the man didn't just honk his horn but instead got out of his vehicle and offered to help.

"Sorry about that," Jeff replied. "I was daydreaming about spring."

"No problem," Kevin replied. "It will be good to get some of this cold weather behind us." With that, he returned to his vehicle.

Jeff put the car in gear and drove on.

Dark Hollow Road was a dirt and gravel road that snaked its way through a canopy of tall pine trees and dense overgrowth. It truly was a typical West Virginia 'hollow.' One got the feeling that they were leaving civilization behind the further along the road they traveled. Jeff immediately regretted not having traded his Lexus in for a pickup truck, which seemed more appropriate given the terrain he had to navigate.

More than once, the car's undercarriage scraped a high spot in the road where the ruts got a little too deep for the car to adequately clear the middle section of the road. With each scrapping sound, Jeff imagined his oil pan being ripped off or his transmission casing getting damaged, causing him some ungodly repair expense when he went to have the vehicle serviced.

However (and despite his worries), the Lexus did make it through the five-mile obstacle course and to the clearing which signified the entrance to the Dark Hollow Mine operation.

Today was his first day on the job. He could have started six months earlier when he got out of jail, but the State allowed him to go on unemployment since he was wrongfully imprisoned, which of course, had cost him his regular job.

Jeff figured he would get as much out of the State as possible, given that he was innocent and they robbed him of his career and eighteen months of his life.

However, the benefits did eventually end and the job offer was coming to a close. So, here he was.

He navigated the muddy Lexus into a parking space outside a Williams Scottsman trailer that had been converted into an office. Kevin Blackthorne's pickup truck pulled into the space beside him.

"Well hell," Kevin called out in a friendly voice as he stepped out of his truck. "I didn't know you were coming to the mines. You must be one of the new guys."

He came over to Jeff, this time to make formal introductions. "The name's, Kevin Blackthorne," Kevin said with an outstretched hand.

Jeff shook the man's hand and replied, "Jeff Abraham. Yes, I am one of the new miners. Today's my first day. Afternoon shift – noon to midnight."

"Same here," Kevin acknowledged. "Hay, you're going to be tearing up that pretty ride of yours if you keep driving up this mud hole."

"I just figured that out," Jeff said.

The two men went into the trailer and Jeff filled out the customary paperwork. There were about twelve men congregating in the room. These men made up the 'newbies' who were starting that day. They would be in the office for about four hours watching some safety videos and then would join a larger crew of about fifty miners who made up the Cassie shift that day.

As Jeff began to watch the first of the films, a loud rumbling of thunder was heard followed by the sounds of a very hard rain. "Hopefully the rain will wash some of the mud off of the Lexus," Jeff thought to himself.

However, as the day went on, the unremitting rain became annoying and ominous. It was very hard to listen to the films with the volume of the rain. As the day progressed, Jeff was reminded of Bridge Creek, already over its banks, and wondered if he would be able to make it out of Dark Hollow at midnight when his shift let out.

Eventually the video watching concluded and each man was issued some work gloves and a yellow hard hat. Then the men moved on to a second supply room where they were issued parkas and rain gear. Men began suiting up.

Tom Williams, a sixty-year-old Scottish mining veteran with a heavy salt-and-pepper-colored beard, noticed the doubtful look in Jeff's face as he put on the raincoat. "Something bothering ya lad?" he asked.

"Well," Jeff replied. "I think it's a bit overkill to have to wear the rain gear when we only have to walk from the offices to the mine entrance."

Tom let out a gut busting laugh that seemed to startle the new miners in the group. "You don't need it for the storm outside," he remarked. "It's the storm inside that you need to worry about!"

One of the new miners, a man who Jeff later found out was named Herman, asked, "Whatcha talking about?"

"There's a lot of make water in this hill," Tom replied. "It's always raining in there. So much in fact that one of you will probably be running the pumps to keep the levels from getting too high."

"I don't think this shit's going to fit me!" came the voice of another new miner, a man name Ben Boyar, whom the crew would call "Bubba." Bubba stood approximately six feet five inches tall and weighed every bit of 320 pounds. The plastic raincoat (although a 2XL and the largest size the company had) looked direly small for the oversized giant. "Ah, fuck it!" he said and handed the uniform back to the company attendant. "If I get wet, I get wet!"

"Oh, you'll get wet all right," Tom replied. "Pretty much every day we have to work with a raincoat, rain pants, and a rain helmet. You'll see, you all will." Tom made a sweeping motion to the newbies. "In just a few minutes down there you all will be soaking wet! They don't call it the Soggy Vein for nothing."

The miners all suited up and went outside. As they approached the entrance to the mine Jeff wondered how much mud, water, and coal dirt he would be trekking into his car. Coming up here he was worried about the outside of his car, now as he approached the gapping whole in the side of the hill, he was thinking about the inside. Little did Jeff realize that he would never see his Lexus LS600 ever again to find out.

***

Clarksburg Telegram
December 23

CLARKSBURG – Forecasters are warning of flash flooding in the area, as above average temperatures over the past week have thawed out much of the snow and ice. Don't look for a white Christmas this year but it will be a wet one. The West Fork River rose from its normal three foot levels on December 19 to twenty-three feet as of December 22. Residents who live near low-lying areas are encouraged to monitor flood levels as rain is forecasted through Christmas day.

CHAPTER 8

It had been a fairly hectic day at work and Jonathan Lake was very happy to call it quits for the day. He was looking forward to having some time off between Christmas Eve and New Year's. It seemed that everybody who came into the car dealership wanted their automobiles detailed and with half the staff gone, it was up to Johnny to work double-hard this holiday season.

Before heading home, his first stop would be O'Malory's, a fine Irish pub along the way. O'Malory's had the coldest Guinness beer on draught and after detailing cars all day, a cold one (or two) was in order.

More than once, he had been offered a promotion at the Buick dealership to salesman, but for Johnny, there was something about detailing cars that kept his mind busy and off other things.

William, his foster child, would be at the Catholic church for a little while and that gave Johnny enough time to zone out and relax over the dark brew before heading home.

O'Malory's was lively, but not too lively. Jonathan really didn't care much for the sports bar atmosphere and O'Malory's was more subdued, dark and Irish.

Being that the holidays were right around the corner, O'Malroy's did have the obligatory Christmas décor, but it still lacked the loud and boisterous music that many of the other bars in the area were known for. And for Johnny, that was a good thing.

"G'day, lad," came the voice of Sammy, the bartender, as Johnny pulled up a stool.

"Howdy," Johnny replied, not trying to hide his American accent.

"Shall I pour you a pint of the usual?" Sammy asked.

Johnny nodded.

Moments later, a frothy glass of dark brew was before him in a frosted mug. Johnny liked his beer cold and the Guinness hit the spot.

He drank it with amazing speed and Sammy was quick to place another before his thirsty patron.

"Much obliged," Johnny said.

Halfway through the second glass, a tall, sultry-looking woman with dark hair and piercing-blue eyes sat down next to Johnny.

"Is this seat taken?" she asked.

"It is now," Johnny remarked in an off-handed way.

The woman ordered a cosmopolitan and moments later, Sammy fulfilled the order.

As the bartender moved away, the woman turned to Johnny and said, "Hello handsome. Do you have a name?"

"John. John Lake," he replied.

She extended a hand, "Amanda Davenport. Actually, I had thought you might be someone else."

Johnny raised an eyebrow.

"I'm actually looking for a man named Jonathan Harker. You bear an uncanny resemblance to him."

Johnny's blood went cold at the sound of his birth name – a name he had hoped to forget. A name that needed to be buried in the past along with all the other shit he did back in the states.

"A lot of people look like other people," was his reply.

Amanda studied his nonverbal communication and Johnny could tell that she was not 100 percent convinced with his reply.

"Tell me, Mr. Lake," Amanda said, "have you ever been to West Virginia?"

Johnny didn't like where this was going. Who was this lady and how in the hell did she find him? "A time or two," he said.

Amanda scooted closer. As she leaned forward to whisper into Johnny's ear, he could not help but notice her amply proportioned rack. D-cups, he would guess, and how the dress she was wearing revealed a tasteful amount of cleavage. As she drew near, he could smell the Chanel No. 9 perfume she had on.

"Listen, I know who you are Mr. Harker. I've been trying to locate you for damn-near three years. I'm William McConnellson's aunt."

"Holy fuck," Johnny whispered back, the blood was draining from his face. Somehow, he had been busted.

"I also know you are on the run and that's why you're in Canada," she said.

"But how…" Johnny started to ask.

Amanda quickly put a finger to his lips. "Hush. I'm not here to blow your cover. I just need some answers, hon. Okay?"

Johnny simply nodded.

"Let's go back to my hotel room. There's some things we need to discuss," Amanda said. "Besides, this place is getting too crowded."

Johnny looked around. Sure enough O'Malory's was starting to pick up. This afternoon was getting a lot more interesting. He paid his tab and headed out with Ms. Davenport.

As they left, he saw Sammy grinning at him out of the corner of his eye.

Fifteen minutes later, they were in Room 327 in the Colfax Holiday Inn.

Amanda motioned him over to sit down on a sofa that was in the room. She put a hand on his knee and said, "I'm so glad William's okay. When his mom died, I was unable to look after him."

Johnny asked the obvious question, "Why?"

"I was in the hospital."

"Hospital?"

"Yes, but not the normal kind," she replied. "I was in Weston."

The Weston State Lunatic Asylum was widely regarded by those in West Virginia as a place where all the nuts lived. Amanda must have caught an expression on Johnny's face.

Her eyes narrowed, "It's not what you think," she said. "I was locked up for nymphomania and masturbation. They thought I was a sexual deviant. My stepdad was the pastor of our local church and one night he and some of the church clergy caught me with a vibrator enjoying myself in the youth building."

Johnny stifled a smile that was quickly rising to his lips as he imagined the scene for a brief moment.

She shook her head. "It really was innocent fun but they made such a big spectacle over it. Before I knew it, I was shipped off to Weston where I spent two years trying to cope with my illness." She raised her index fingers in the air making quote symbols as she mentioned the word 'illness.'

Amanda paused for a moment. Her face went blank as she recalled being under Dr. Cane's care. Every morning, her bra and panties would be removed and she would be strapped to an examination table where she was forced to undergo electroconvulsive therapy – or ECT – as he called it.

"Now, now Miss Davenport," Dr. Cane would say in an ever-so-sweet voice. "Time for your morning ECT." He always said it in a tickled voice, like an old friend bringing the morning's coffee.

"I told your stepdad about the progress we were making," he would often remark. Deep down, she knew Cane was a sadist. She wondered if this was true at all because ever since her mother died, her stepfather never seemed to care much for her.

She doubted he even spoke with the 'good doctor' at all because he never came around once since she had been admitted.

In addition to placing the shock pads on her temples, Dr. Cane would strap electrodes on the young lady's nipples and vagina. He used small amounts of KY Jelly to help the pads stay in place. The cold gel never failed to make her nipples grow involuntarily erect. Dr. Cane always made sure to pause just a moment on each nipple to make sure the gel would get worked into the skin.

Like clockwork, the nurses would leave the room and let the evil doctor work by himself. The moment they were alone, his voice would change into a menacing growl. "I think deep down, you like this, don't you, Miss Davenport?"

She knew better not to answer him. "Yes, I think you like having your little pussy shocked." With that, the first wave of shocks would blast through her, rocking her body and bringing it momentarily off the bed. If it weren't for the straps, she knew she would be thrown clear off it.

She screamed. He hit her again with the electric current. Often she would pass out. During her 'blackouts,' she dreamt he was standing over her, not as a human, but with demonic, glowing eyes. In these dreams, she was not wearing any clothes and the hospital room would somehow transform into a dirty factory basement – a macabre, hellish scene, in fact.

She would dream she was on a metal work table and being held down by someone. In reality, it was the straps, of course, but in the dream, she imagined hearing Dr. Cane yell out. "Hold her down, brother. Make sure the bitch doesn't move!"

In vain, she would struggle but it was no use. Every dream was the same: the Dr. Cane in the dream was not the human Dr. Cane in the hospital. This Dr. Cane was part man and part machine. The lower part of his body looked alien, almost android. He would stand over her with an erect machine-like penis and rape her. With each thrust, electric shocks shot through her loins with a terrible pain mixed with an undercurrent of pleasure. She would wail, but it did not stop the torture.

Eventually, she would wake up and be in a simple hospital bed back in her room.

"Amanda, are you okay?" It was Johnny. He was leaning close to her face, examining her for responsiveness. For a few moments, she must have spaced out. *Damn,* she thought.

"I'm sorry," she said. "I was just thinking about the first time I was committed to Weston. I was seventeen."

Strangely enough, her nipples had become erect and they were obvious through her silk dress. She saw Johnny inadvertently looking at them. He really wasn't trying, but couldn't help it being that he was so close to her.

There was a strong tension in the room. Amanda knew she had to break it and get things back on track. "Wanna fuck?"

***

While Jonathan and Amanda were becoming better acquainted in Room 327 of the Colfax Holiday Inn, William McConnellson III was praying the rosary in Colfax Abbey, a local Catholic Church and monastery.

William had never been a religious boy, at least not until six months ago. That's when everything changed.

Before then, Willie was a misunderstood, rebellious kid who was placed into foster care at an early age and eventually left to the state's care at the West Virginia Industrial Home For Troubled Youth.

But those days seemed long ago, an eternity in fact. Although it had been only two years since he last stepped foot in the juvenile detention center – or more aptly put, since he burnt it down – he never had a real sense of good and evil.

That however changed with his last visit to West Virginia. He would never be the same and although he never really got to know Father Alex as a religious leader, he realized that there was a man of God. Father Alex had known age-old truths that in the end saved him and Jonathan from certain peril.

That fateful night, Father Alex gave his life when the three of them fought off Victor Rothenstein and two vampire queens. That scene would be forever burned into young William's memory.

When the two of them returned to their home in Colfax minus Father Alex, William half expected his tutor Chloe Ashburn, who was a nun at the abbey and close friend to Father Alex, to abandon him. However, Chloe accepted their unbelievable story at face value and offered William some work at the monastery.

William took solace in this and began actively pursuing a relationship with Jesus Christ and learning about the church.

As he prayed, he thought about Amanda, who he always called "Mandy" as a boy. Mandy was his last living relative and he found her one day on Facebook. He knew it was a risk telling her he was still alive, as most thought he had been killed when the youth center exploded. Many died that night, although only William and Jonathan knew that it wasn't the fire that had killed those inside.

He shuddered. Even years later, the scene still haunted him. The scene of a winged, bat-like demon raping and killing all those in the cafeteria -- what a massacre!

In fact, Jonathan's girlfriend died that night. William knew her well. Miss Lucy was a good lady and had always treated William well.

William realized he was trembling. He looked at the rosary beads with tears in his eyes. So many people were hurt that night, but Jonathan and he made it right, didn't they? He hoped so.

After getting their wits, they returned to West Virginia to dispense justice. Father Alex VanHelsen was with them. Yes, they succeeded in killing all three vampires in the Madison House that night. Hell, they even succeeded in burning that accursed place down.

As the beads moved along his fingers, William prayed for solace. *We did kill them, didn't we?*

He felt that they did, however there was something still bothering him about the whole ordeal: Father Alex insisted that they destroy an obelisk that had sat about a mile from the old Madison House.

This was a bizarre diversion and the structure was abnormally resilient to their busting on it with sledgehammers. They did bust some of it up, but not all. William shook his head. It seemed so strange that Father Alex assert they attack that thing first *before* fighting the vampires.

William silently wondered that had they went to the Madison House during the day, it would have been easier to defeat the vampires. However, they spent way too much time on the old obelisk.

And the obelisk destroyed the car, didn't it? It delayed them. Yes it had. It had delayed them long enough for the sun to set and the vampires to wake up from their dead slumber.

What was it about that obelisk? William thought.

Father Alex had told them about it being a gateway to Hades and a channel for demonic forces to walk the earth.

They did destroy it, didn't they? William certainly hoped so.

***

Amanda Davenport was amazing in bed, simply amazing. It had been two long years since Jonathan had been with a woman and at times he wondered if he would ever feel like screwing again. He had developed feelings for Lucy Westerna in the short time he knew her. But she died and left him with emotional scars that continued to haunt him even to this day.

Amanda's luscious boobs bounced in glorious splendor in the hotel room mirror as Johnny took her from behind. He grabbed a handful of her long, dark hair and gave it a firm tug.

"Shit yeah!" she screamed.

Johnny fucked her harder. With each slapping of his hips into her perfectly-rounded ass, she moaned loudly with pleasure. Johnny was enjoying this immensely.

He reached around and began fingering her very moist pussy lips. Her pubic mound was nicely trimmed, he noted as his fingers brushed over the coarse surface. Smiling, he also noted that this was one girl that needed no lubrication. He felt her dripping with erotic nectar. He massaged her quickly and in sync with his thrusts. She squealed, enjoying his technique very much.

Looking back towards the mirror, a cross she was wearing around her neck bounced widely from her neck to her tits. For a split second, Johnny's tormented brain took him back to the night he battled the vampires in the Madison House.

That night, William had been carrying an alabaster crucifix. In the pitch-black basement, it was the one thing that glowed. The glow was faint, but it was there, nevertheless. The cross looked as if it had a radioactive quality about it. Perhaps it did, as it burnt Victor Rothenstein like a branding iron when William struck him with it. It was radioactive with the Holy Spirit.

"Oh God, I'm going to cum!" Amanda screamed. This broke Johnny's daydream and brought him right back to the present-day activities at hand.

Seconds later, she wailed upwards and back into Johnny. In the mirror, Johnny could see her squirt a torrent of feminine juices over the other side of the bed and beyond.

Johnny had never been with a squirter before and was taken by surprise at how radically turned on he was at the sight of this.

He immediately found himself ejaculating with such force that momentarily he thought he was going to blackout.

Amanda turned to embrace Johnny and the two lovers fell to the bed. For the next several minutes, they kissed passionately.

That was one heck of an introduction, Johnny thought to himself as he caressed the nude Venus before him.

Some undetermined time later, Johnny's cell phone went off; it was William.

"Hello Jonathan," William said. "I was wondering if you wanted me to bring back something for dinner or should I get something out for myself only?"

"Let's eat in tonight," Johnny replied. "I ran into your aunt and she'll be joining us this evening." Johnny shot a glance at Amanda who was lying on the bed. She smiled.

There was a brief silence on the phone. "My aunt's in town? Mandy?"

"You mean Amanda?" Johnny corrected.

"Yes. But I've always called her Mandy even as a little boy. I can't believe she actually came!"

Boy did she ever, Johnny thought to himself. Now it was his turn to smile back at his lover. "Yep, she came champ," he replied. "She's with me now. We're picking up some things from her hotel and we'll be home soon."

"Okay, great!" William was noticeably excited. "I'll see you guys soon!"

As he hung up, Johnny looked at Amanda and said, "It sounds like William is really happy you came up here."

"I'm glad I found Willie," she said. "There have been so many times I was missing from his life. Other than you, I am all he has. I am glad that I now have the means to be more active in his life."

Johnny thought about asking her more about this, but decided to save it for another time. That statement implied all sorts of things: from her stay as a psychiatric patient in Weston to a different financial perspective. Some questions are better saved for later.

As the two dressed and left the hotel, over an inch of snow had covered their vehicles. It seemed to be snowing hard and heavy.

"Gotta love these Canadian winters," Johnny remarked.

"Actually, West Virginia winters are kind of bad. I don't know if I like this at all," Amanda remarked.

"I have a four wheel drive," Johnny replied. "We could go in it."

"That's cool," Amanda said. "My Porsche may not go too well in the snow."

The 911 Carrera was white to begin with and now could barely be made out underneath the frosty blanket of powder.

"Come on," Johnny grinned as he motioned to his Ford F-150. "Let's take the old standby."

In a few minutes, the two were on the road and heading back to Johnny's and William's trailer. Amanda had informed him that she worked for a large pharmaceutical company in Morgantown, West Virgina, as a sales rep and things were doing well for her.

She also explained how Willie, as she liked to call her nephew, befriended her on Facebook and gave her an open invitation to come sometime and visit.

"I was shocked – but in a good way – when I found out Willie was still alive," Amanda said. "I am so glad he got out of that God-awful place."

"He seems like a really good kid," Johnny replied. "Quiet and thoughtful."

"Oh, he is," Amanda said. "He's very bright. He just needed a better home life – that's all."

Johnny nodded. He remembered the night he rescued William from the West Virginia Industrial Home For Troubled Youth. The place was ablaze and William was trapped. In fact, Johnny's F-150 still had a smashed in bumper from where he rammed the building's locked doors to help him escape. That night had been the start of the *strange days* for Jonathan Harker, or Johnny Lake, as he was known in Canada.

"Well, I tried to give him a fresh start," Johnny remarked. "With the school burning down, there would be all sorts of police problems. We thought it best to start again; both of us."

"I know exactly where you're coming from," Amanda said.

Johnny wasn't really sure if she know *exactly* where he was coming from. That night, Johnny had seen a large winged demon vampire descend on the school/prison. The very winged demon moments later had killed his new girlfriend and slaughtered all those inside – all except William. William managed to save himself and kill the beast by engaging the prison's automatic lockdown controls and setting the place on fire, trapping the demon vampire inside. Yes, that was just the beginning of Jonathan and William's 'partnership.'

Nowadays, William McConnellson III was William Lake, Johnny's son. The two played the role well and left it at that. No one except Chole Ashburn knew their real identities and she kept the matter secret. At least that was until Aunt Mandy came on the scene.

One thing was for certain, things were starting to get interesting.

CHAPTER 9

MELAS, WEST VIRGINIA
U.S.A.

Margaret Brite scratched around in total darkness. All traces of time and the life she knew were no more. There were others like her – that much her darkened mind could comprehend – but that was all it could do.

It had been years since she had last eaten anything. It had been nearly four years since she had been alive. A religious girl, Maggie, as she liked to be called, couldn't fathom why now she was in a place of perpetual darkness, perpetual torment.

When she was first killed, she remembered that fateful night in vivid detail. Now, all memories including that one were no more.

That night – over two years ago – Maggie was walking home from church. She had met one of the nicest men – TC – at the service. TC had offered her a ride home, but she refused. She liked walking.

Her home was only about a mile from the church and this was a common ritual for her. She had just left the church parking lot when she noticed a white sedan idling along the edge of the road.

She really thought nothing of it at the time. Behind the driver's seat was an older man. She had seen him around town. He was the man who ran the antiques shop. Pinkman was his name. He was part owner of Pinkman and Rothenstein in downtown Melas.

"Excuse me, Miss?" Mr. Pinkman yelled to Maggie. "I noticed you dropped something back there in the parking lot as you were leaving church."

"Really?" Maggie said with surprise. "I didn't think I had."

She looked around and sure enough her purse was missing. *How in the world did I drop that?* she wondered to herself as she approached the sedan.

As if from out of nowhere, TC stepped in front of her and produced her purse. "You should really be more careful," he advised. An evil grin had appeared on his lips.

Before she realized it, Pinkman jumped out of the car and hit her with something. She really never got a look at the object, but realized she was being shocked badly before she passed out.

Walter Pinkman had used a stun gun on Maggie Brite that night. As she fell to the ground, TC was quick to grab her and get her into the car before someone saw them.

Walt and TC drove quickly to the Madison House on Raccoon Run Road. The master of the abode would be waiting their arrival.

The 'master' was Victor Rothenstein, Walter Pinkman's partner in the antiques business and lord of death. Rothenstein was an age-old vampire. Pinkman and TC would help ensure Rothenstein was fed regularly with fresh victims. In return, Rothenstein kept them supplied with money and resources to live very comfortably.

Maggie vaguely remembered being dragged through the Madison House's back yard as she slowly regained consciousness.

Suddenly, a dark figure shadowed the doorway. Tall and carnivorous, Victor Rothenstein could be described as both brutally handsome and sickly pale at the same time. His long fingers curled around the doorframe, like a spider examining his prey.

Maggie screamed, "I recognize all three of you! When I get out of here, I'm going straight to the police."

Victor let out a laugh that carried with it a chill that froze her very soul. "You can try, my dear. But that won't be necessary."

He inched forward onto the porch. Maggie's heart pounded with such force she thought it would explode in her chest. She tried to move, but Walter and TC had a firm grip on her that prevented her from fleeing.

"Lower your resistance," Victor commanded in a low and somehow seductive voice. "Release your will." The voice was somewhat hypnotic; it could not be argued with.

He moved within inches of her face. The monster was so close, so real. Her mind pleaded with her to get away, to somehow escape, but she knew that was no longer an option. She now had no choice but to endure what was to come.

She watched with horror and fascination as his lips curled into a smile; a smile that revealed razor-sharp, pointed teeth.

She gasped and struggled some more. His teeth – those god-awful teeth – glistened with saliva. These were teeth that demanded blood – her blood. His eyes shot toward her neck. He wanted the vein.

No longer in control of her will, she bent her neck, revealing the vein toward her. "That's a good girl," he said. "Just relax. This will only hurt for a moment."

Incredibly sharp, searing pain flooded her, but it was quickly replaced by a wave of euphoria. She felt a strong, sexual sensation wash over her. Simultaneously, her head felt light and she began to faint from loss of blood.

Victor sucked on her neck with careful accuracy, not letting any blood go to waste. Her body became limp and eventually sagged back into TC's and Walter's arms.

"Good job boys," Victor said when it was all over. "That one was still a virgin. Her blood was ever so sweet."

Looking at Walter he said, "You know what to do."

"Yes sir," Walter replied. "I'll take her over to Jimbo for clean up."

"Wait a second, Walt," TC replied. "Are you sure that's a good idea? After Jimbo burnt down the chopping house, where's he going to do his work?"

"Let's not concern the master with the incidentals," Walt replied. He looked at Victor who was watching the two carefully, "Jimbo won't be a problem, sir."

"He better not be, we pay that silly fuck enough."

"I couldn't agree more," Walter replied.

The two men put the body back into the white sedan and drove to Jimbo's residence on North Coat Street.

Jimbo's house had a driveway with heavy brush and weeds growing along the edge of the property. This allowed their car to back into the driveway and get the body out without the neighbors noticing. Jimbo's large Lincoln was also in the driveway.

The two men got out and carried the body to Jimbo's back porch. "Should we just stick her in the Lincoln's trunk?" TC asked.

"Hell no," Walter replied. "Jimbo needs to cut off her head! We don't want her coming back, now do we?"

"Just a thought," TC commented.

A startled Jimbo met them around back. "Dudes, I thought we were done with this," he said, looking at the girl and shaking his head with disapproval.

"We're done when *he* says we're done," TC replied.

Jimbo anxiously looked around to see if any of his neighbors were watching. "Okay boys, get out of here. I'll take care of it."

Walter and TC pulled out quickly, leaving Jimbo and Maggie's corpse behind.

As soon as they were out of sight, Jimbo popped open the trunk to his Lincoln, laid a sheet of plastic down and put her body in the car. "Damned if I'll be chopping her head off!" he said to himself.

Jimbo Whilders was one of the few people who possessed a key to the gate of the abandoned Runners Ride Mining property. Sure, people such as hunters and partiers would find ways to wander onto the property from time to time, but most never came clear down to where the entrance was. That section was gated well and very private.

Jimbo unlocked the gate, pulled forward, and then closed and locked it behind him. His standard operating procedure was to get the car as close to the entrance of the mine as possible and out of sight of anyone who might accidently come on the mining road, hoist the body into a man-cart, and wheel it down to a large hole about 300 yards or so into the mountain. Once he got to the hole, he dropped the victims over the edge and it was all finished. He never knew how deep the pit was, only that he never heard any of the bodies hit bottom – and he always listened for that.

All the prior victims had been decapitated. Maggie was the first to go over intact. As he lifted her up and out of the man-cart, he thought he saw her chest rise. "Aw, shit!" he exclaimed.

"Don't worry missy, it won't be the fall that kills ya, but the sudden stop at the bottom!" With that, he threw her over head first into the abyss.

Maggie had the slightest sensation of falling, but she was so close to death, that she didn't know if she were dreaming it or not. In reality, her body fell an amazing distance, however before she reached the bottom, her face bounced off a rock protrusion, stabbing her in the left eye. Her decent adjusted with this impact and she finally landed on a pile of rotting bodies. She was dead at this point, or so she thought.

A few days later she 'awoke' delusional and hungry. *Where am I?* she wondered.

The stench of death and decay was overwhelming. This should have stopped the hunger, but it didn't. She was in total darkness and not sure at all what happened to her.

She was unaware that she had turned undead. Had she been on the surface and been able to feed, she would have fully turned into a vampire. However, she was trapped in a mine where she would remain for years, unable to drink the blood of the living.

Eventually Maggie Brite was no more. She existed, but not as Maggie Brite or as a vampire. As time, darkness, and the lust for blood overtook her mind, she became simply a hungry ghoul deep in the dark.

Every few days for the next few months, others were thrown down next to her. They too became mindless ghouls – trapped forever in a black prison – groaning, bouncing into each other from time to time, and scratching at the ever-so-steep walls that trapped them. Yes, they were trapped forever, or so it seemed.

CHAPTER 10

Tom Williams was right. It rained like a waterfall in the deep. Jeff, Bubba, and Herman were part of the newbies assigned to Kevin Blackthorn and Tom Williams. This team would be working in the Creek Slope that evening.

For the first ten minutes within the mine, the men rode in a small mine car deep into the belly of the mountain.

Along the way, Kevin pointed out various identifiers that the men could use to find their way back to the main shaft leading to the surface if they ever became separated from the more seasoned veterans.

At one point, the men came across a locked wooden door with a DO NOT ENTER sign attached to it. Kevin stopped the mine car at this point and the men got out.

"This," he said, "is a cross-tunnel to the Runners Ridge Mine. That mine was closed for safety reasons decades ago because of the steep drops and unexpected pockets of dangerous mine gas. Leave this door closed."

"Lots of men were killed in Runners Ridge back in the day," Tom added. "In fact, mine safety officials about went ape shit when they discovered the cross-tunnel hadn't been permanently sealed off. We'll get around to it one of these days."

Kevin added, "Tom was one of the men who dug the cross-tunnel. He was working on making a supply room, as we are a good ways into the mountain, when he punched through to the other mine shaft."

"Don't remind me," Tom said. "I thought I was going to lose my job when I found I had actually breached the other mine. But that's not the worst part."

"What do you mean?" Jeff asked.

"Well, I call it the Howling Shaft because there were terrible sounds coming from within the deep. Moans and shit."

Bubba's eyes got really wide as Tom described it. Jeff wondered if the old Scottsman wasn't pulling the big guy's leg.

Tom continued, "There were wailing sounds. Freaked me out, I'll readily admit. I quickly got Kevin to agree to let me board it up."

Kevin tried to sooth the story over. "What Tom is describing is the sound of air as it passes through various parts of the mine. When the cross-tunnel was opened, the wind made very odd howling sounds that frightened many of the men working on the supply room that day. Obviously, we couldn't keep a cross-tunnel to Runners Ridge open, so we used a spare door and sealed the entrance. We needed to do this anyway because when we updated the maps, mine regulators wanted to know why we breached the other passage."

Herman and Bubba nodded and both seemed relieved. Jeff shrugged and took Kevin's story at face value.

Kevin changed the subject and began walking along a narrow passage to the left, beyond the door. "Continue this way, gentleman," he gestured.

"This marks the beginning of the Creek Slope," Tom said.

Jeff quickly learned that the Creek Slope was aptly named because the shaft tunneled its way close to Bridge Creek, but stopped a few hundred feet short of actually going under the waterway.

The water, which had been dripping on the men from overhead, seemed to be getting harder and faster the further into the tunnel they walked.

The men passed a pumping station that was chugging along. "This is what gets the make water out of the shaft," Tom said.

Jeff learned that 'make water' was ordinary mine drainage that had to be pumped from the mine.

"Water has always presented serious problems here on the Creek Slope," Kevin said. "In fact, for every ton of coal we mine, we remove over ten tons of water."

"Ten TONS?" Jeff asked skeptically.

"Ten point five if you really must know," Kevin replied. "Just look around you."

Jeff couldn't deny it was really raining in the shaft. The men trudged forward in their raingear for several more unpleasantly damp minutes until they reached their destination.

Some equipment was placed next to a wall up ahead and the men knew this was where they would be working. Even in the dim light of the mine, they could tell they were standing in a rich vein of coal. The black rock glistened wetly along the walls and ceiling of the shaft, as water dripped over it.

Each man was given a pick and shovel and they went to work. The area they were in was extremely narrow and Kevin explained that they needed to manually expand this section so that a conveyer could eventually be installed. Until then, they would have to clear the area manually and extract the coal by hand.

Bubba was given the responsibility of busting through the larger seams and the other men would shovel the coal into a dumpster-like hand cart that would be used to pull it back to where the larger mine car was parked.

Bubba was amazing and strong and heaved the pick with great skill. Both Tom and Kevin were impressed at what large chunks he was able to bust out of the wall.

Sometime before the men's lunch break, Bubba chipped a piece of coal from the ceiling as he was swinging the pick in an overhead arch. Suddenly, there was a loud creaking sound.

Tom had no more than looked up to see where the sound was coming from when the roof gave way.

Herman was killed instantly when rock and water plummeted down on his head. Bubba, Jeff, Kevin, and Tom reflexively jumped back the split second when they saw the roof go and began a rapid sprint up the passageway towards where the mine car was parked.

What the mining company failed to realize was that the survey they were using was inaccurate. The men had been working on an anticline under Bridge Creek and with the recent rains Bridge Creek was flooded well beyond its banks. The men had breached the river!

Water poured into the mine at an astounding pace. The sheer force of the wall of liquid pressed up against the men as they moved further away from the breach site.

Light bulbs that had been strung along the shaft began busting off. Jeff became fearful that he would get electrocuted, but with the water coming in so fast, that was the least of his worries.

Even though the men were fast, they were not fast enough to make it to the mine car before the water got to it. By the time they reached the vehicle, the water was already above the engine compartment. They piled into the mine car as Kevin turned the keys. The car would not start.

Suddenly, the water lifted the mine car and carried it swiftly down the mine shaft. The mine car was not amphibious, but the sheer volume and current of the water flooded the mine shaft like a path of raging rapids. The walls thundered like Niagara Falls.

Big chucks of ice began flooding the cave. These were from the outside river and now posed yet another threat in the dark.

"Holy fuck, we've got to get off this thing!" Tom shouted.

The men followed Tom's lead as he dove off the mine car. They were about eighty yards from where they started and Tom was determined to get further UP the shaft than down it.

"If we stay here, we're going to be drowned!" he screamed above the raging torrent. The frigid water was already up to chest level.

"Get to the Runners Ridge cross-tunnel," Kevin yelled. "Runners Ridge is a higher elevation. If we can get that door open and re-seal it once we're through, we'll have a chance."

"Agreed!" Tom said as the crew pressed forward. "There's not enough time for us to walk all the way back to the Dark Hollow entrance!" The water was coming in fast and furious. The Runners Ridge shaft was indeed their only hope.

Through fierce effort and determination, they made it back against the current to where the DO NOT ENTER door was. Tom didn't wait for Kevin to find a key. He grabbed an axe – one of the many mining tools that frequented the walls at various points along the mining operation – and busted the pad lock off the front of it. "Get in and close the door quick!" he said as he opened it.

The men poured into the small shaft and Tom and Bubba pushed with all their strength against the current to get the door shut again.

Water was coming from underneath the door, but it did provide a temporary reprieve to allow the men a small moment to think as to how they were going to address their predicament.

The men frantically looked around and there was no way to bar the door to reinforce it against the current. They only had seconds to decide what to do next.

Kevin spoke first, "Men, we have to go back through the Runners Ridge Shaft, this door ain't going to hold!" There was no disputing this and they all poured single-file up the narrow cross-tunnel. A loud creaking sound came from behind. He was right: the door would not last for much longer.

The cross-tunnel ended in a small crawlspace that had been hand-dug decades before. The men had to craw on all fours along the seam to wherever it may lead.

The inevitable thought on all their minds was the fact that it would not take water too long to drown them within the narrow confines of this earlier shaft. They could only hope that Kevin's assessment was correct and that somehow they were traveling upwards in the mountain and not further down.

The crawl eventually led them to an eight-foot-wide chamber that stretched for about thirty feet and branched off. The men stood and observed their surroundings.

"Old-style pillar construction," Tom noted as he pointed to how the walls were cut. Room-and-pillar mining involved driving tunnel-like openings to divide the coal seam into rectangular or square blocks. These blocks of coal, or pillars, were sized to provide support for the overlying strata.

"Guys, it's going to be like a checkerboard in here, with pillars between the entrances." Kevin said. "We're going to have to walk along and try to determine where the surface shaft is located."

"Do you mean we are close to the 'entrance'?" Bubba asked, picking up on Kevin's description of the older room and pillar shaft design.

"No, Bubba," Kevin said. "What I meant was the spaces between the pillars are called entrances. It's the same as tunnel."

Bubba nodded, but a stark confusion and worry were in his eyes.

"We're sort of like rats in a maze," Jeff observed.

"That's an accurate assessment," Tom replied.

The men made it about 100 feet or so up this path before they came to an old saw-horse style barricade. The word "DANGER" was attached on the saw-horse. Shortly beyond this was a drop-off.

"Damn!" Kevin said. "We went the wrong way."

To compound the anxiety, a loud cracking noise could be heard from behind the men followed by a loud pop.

"The door gave way!" Tom said. The men knew water would be coming into the shaft in moments.

It didn't take more than a minute before water begun swirling around their feet and moving past them and down the tunnel. They watched anxiously as water poured past the barricade and over the drop-off.

"Boys, I don't know how deep that chasm is or how long it will be before the water floods this place." Kevin said. "We've got to keep moving and looking for another way out. If we can't find the main exit, maybe we can locate an air shaft or something."

Jeff was glad that at least one of them seemed to have a level head, because he was slowly starting to lose his.

Suddenly, a loud moan was heard from beyond the barricade – somewhere from deep within the abyss.

"Shit! What was that?" Jeff exclaimed.

"The Howling Shaft!" Tom yelled in reply.

"Come on," Kevin said, dismissing the banter. "I said we've got to keep moving!"

The men went down another chamber with blind hope that they would have a better outcome. This time, they came to an enclave in the pillar that had an old table, on top of which lay a mining map.

"Thank God!" Kevin said as he ran over to the table. He brought his miners light close to the faded pages and the men glanced at each other.

"I don't know how in the hell you are going to read that thing, Kevin." Tom said.

He was right. The map was covered in about an inch of coal dust. The paper was also deteriorating and in a very unstable condition. Kevin blew on the table, sending a plume of black dust into the spaces beyond. Bubba coughed reflexively as the air was polluted with the new dust.

For people that had to be moving along, it seemed to take an eternity for Kevin to make out what the map was saying. Tom started to get impatient, "Give me that thing!" he said, pulling at a corner of the map. It disintegrated in his hands.

"You dumbass!" Kevin yelled. "You can't move it! Can't you see? It pulls apart!"

Tom sadly shook his head. Kevin was right.

"Guys," Kevin started, "the best I can tell is that the large hole back there is the opposite side of a hole near the main exit of the old mine.

"Back when this place was operational, they kept tunneling around it and kept finding more holes. This entire place is very dangerous. No wonder they shut it down.

"Another few hundred feet down this shaft we are presently in may lead us around that hole. No guarantees, as fuck nut here ripped off half the map."

"Go to hell, Kevin," Tom replied angrily.

"What choices do we have?" Jeff asked, feeling an increasing sense of urgency.

"None," growled Kevin, scowling at Tom, before returning his glare to the remnants of the map, squinting down and wiping off coal-dust, but determined to commit every line to memory. The map was clearly too fragile to pick up, and Kevin wanted to recall as much detail as possible.

Kevin looked up to warn, "Mines with water running through can be dangerous. The oxygen gets taken out of the water as it rushes through the rock before it even gets to the mine workings. The oxygen-depleted water pulls oxygen out of the air as it flows through the mine workings, so there might be low levels of oxygen - which can be fatal."

Bubba's eyes widened to white circles in his big, grimy face, "Face the floods, or face whatever's moanin' down there in that hell-hole. Either way, we're gonna die, right?"

Kevin turned his burning head torch towards Bubba, blinding him, "Think like that, and you will, boy! I told you - it's only the wind, for fuck's sake!"

"Aye- and there's many a bad case of wind killing a man..." sneered the veteran, Tom. Nobody was in a mood to find that comment humorous.

Jeff wanted to run. Anywhere. He hadn't spent almost two years in jail to die here like a rat in a trap, and he jiggled one leg in irritation and impatience, before bursting out in desperation, "Then let's go! Tom - you worked on this shaft. You must have some idea of where we can go. Help us!"

Tom cupped his forehead in his palms, tilting his hard hat backwards, "Now you just wait a second, rookie. Yes I punched through to this side of the old mine, but I never took a leisurely stroll around in here taking in the scenery. Remember the noises?" He scratched his head, "Shit! Don't you think I've tried to forget everything about this area? Fuck knows!"

In a fit of decisiveness, Kevin strode towards the incline, and turned towards the others, "Come on. Where there's wind, eventually, there is air. Call it Runner's Ridge if it sits prettier with you that way, but the Howling Shaft it is."

116

"For better or worse," added Tom, and the others followed them both, to wherever fate would take them.

With water running constantly over their ankles in a shallow stream, they shunted the old saw-horse aside, the 'DANGER' sign mocking them behind their backs as they side-stepped towards the rock face to one side of the drop-off, where a rocky outcrop was raised above the waters. Tom nodded the beam of his head-torch towards the other side of the chasm, picking up shadowy ridges in the pitch black.

"There's another shaft off in that direction, as far as I can tell, but subsidence has crumbled the path away. If we can make our own way over there, I reckon we can meet up with the secondary shaft again, a ways down."

The others scanned the direction in which he pointed, unable to make out much more than a few feet ahead of them with the focused lights on their helmets. What they could make out filled them with dread.

"Fuck. Shit," said Bubba.

To the right of the drop-off, which was already increasing in torrents, the muddy ridge of slippery rock beneath their feet, three feet wide, tapered away over the abyss to something the width of the ball of a foot. And that was as far as they could see, so God knows what happened after that - a sheer drop into infinity was quite likely.

"Isn't there another way?" asked Jeff, picking up on Bubba's rapid breathing behind him as the giant panicked in the awareness that his huge frame was neither aerodynamic nor agile enough to face this tightrope walking feat of balance.

"No, there isn't!" yelled Kevin, and pressed on ahead.

"He's right, laddie," the old Scot conceded, "Much as I hate to say it, it's likely our only way out."

He patted Bubba on his drenched shirt shoulder, "If you've still got any tools on you, use them for leverage. Ever ridden a motorbike, son?"

Bubba nodded, bewildered, as Tom went on: "Compensate for the bend, and lean into it. Don't look down, lean into the wall and pretend you've got all the time and space in the world."

Kevin had already begun to edge his way along the thin ledge, and swiftly followed his own momentum, hugging the wall of rock, and tiptoeing delicately but quickly across the space. By the time he was just outside their torch beams reach, he yelled, and turned his helmet their way, forming a beacon of hope.

"It's okay! It widens here! You only have about thirty feet to get across to reach safety!"

Safety! If only they had known what 'safety' lay ahead for them, they would not be defining it as such. Kevin was nearly jubilant, and buoyed up by his success,

Jeff was next. As he started making his way toward Kevin in the distance, he noticed his feet growing numb from the dampness. Random thoughts ran through his head reflecting how the water in mines is often deep and can be dangerously cold; filling an area with steep sides as it did, it would be hard to climb out. "Don't slip!" his racing mind keep telling him as he crossed the ledge. What lay ahead was hard to tell.

Jeff made his way across, wavering slightly mid-way, but using his small hand pick to wedge into the fissures in the rocky walls, to give him extra security.

Kevin looked like he was standing in a puddle. Even apparently shallow water can deceptively cover drop-offs, sharp objects, and other dangers. More pervasive still, a wet mine can rust metalwork, or rot timbers, shoring and ladders, making conditions more hazardous. Jeff shuddered in the cold, silently praying for his mind to remain calm.

They both turned their head-torches in the direction Bubba would come from, picking out the ledge for him, and tracing the pathway he would take.

"Hey Bubba! It's easy!" Jeff lied, bulling him up. He edged back out along the far end of the ledge and reached out a hand towards Bubba to make the distance appear shorter.

Bubba stood transfixed part-way across the ledge, just before it got really narrow, Tom standing behind him with his hands lightly on his shoulders, muttering words of wisdom.

Suddenly, above the rush of water and the sound of the foaming waterfall below, they heard another loud, extended moan. From the corner of his eye, Jeff saw what must be grey tree trunks flash by in the river water below the drop-off, but they seemed to wave branches out, like arms. Bundles of rags. And the howling. His mind was playing tricks on him, for sure.

119

Bubba wavered and wobbled, glassy-eyed, and it was all old Tom could do to steady him. He muttered more urgently in his ear, "Okay, Bubba, lad. Stand firm, like a rock. Keep to the rock, like a magnet."

"It's only the wind!" yelled Jeff, across the cavernous space, his existence merely one of two fuzzy dots of light in the distance.

"And the old iron gates!" Kevin joined in, "They're creaking under the weight of water!"

"You can see gates?" Jeff asked, excited by the hope that they were back on track to the outside world.

"No," replied Kevin, "I'm just giving the guy something to live for."

Bubba pressed his face into the damp rock face, breathing heavily and stepped daintily sidewise like a massive ballerina, Tom following closely beside him, urging him gently all the way. When Bubba's foot slipped, sending a rock crashing down below, bouncing off the rocks beneath, Tom whispered to him to concentrate only on his voice, and carry on. Before he knew it, Jeff was fumbling his hand to his shirt sleeve and pulling him home to the wider ledge. Bubba was bundled into the back of a sort of open cave, while Tom was grabbed and hauled in to safety.

All four gasped a sigh of relief, and looked back at the way they had come before facing what lay ahead.

Kevin laughed, "Thank fuck for..." He was suddenly felled to the ground by a black shadow that swung out of the darkness with a spine-chilling howl.

CHAPTER 11

One of the few people who didn't treat Bobby Luellan like he was some kind of a nut was Marcel. Marcel was a Colombian migrant worker who helped with chores at a nearby milk farm next to Bobby's trailer park in Wolf Summit.

Lately, Marcel had been going on and on about 'El Chupacabra' a winged, bat-like creature that had been spotted terrorizing the local farms. All of the migrant workers were afraid of El Chupacabra.

"The farm owners don't believe us," Marcel had confided during one conversation with Bobby. "But they don't know what we know!"

Bobby looked at Marcel with wind-eyed astonishment. "What is a Chupacabra?"

"In Columbia, El Chupacabra is a most feared creature. It is a vampire!

"Growing up in Vereda Angosturas, there was said to be a creature of the night – El Chupacabra. If fed on the livestock – it drank their blood.

The villagers struck a deal with El Chupacabra and gave it a portion of the town's livestock in exchange..." Marcel's voice trailed off.

"In exchange for what?" Bobby asked.

"In exchange for our lives!" Marcel replied. He looked white as a ghost.

It appeared as if Marcel had swallowed his tongue, but after a while, he continued, "I never thought there could be more than one. I never thought it would be here in America. This is bad, Gringo, very bad."

"The farm owners don't believe us," Marcel repeated. "They think we are killing the livestock and blaming it on El Chupacabra. All of the farms around have been hit. The Chupacabra doesn't take the meat, it drinks the blood, Gringo, it drinks the blood!"

Bobby found himself salivating at the thought of the dead animals and wondered out loud, "What do they do with the meat?"

"You mean after El Chupacabra is done with it?" Marcel asked.

Bobby shook his head affirmatively.

"You can't eat it Gringo," he replied. "It can't be eaten. Meat's tainted. We have to bury the dead animals."

"Sounds like a waste to me," Bobby replied. "It's a sin to waste meat."

"You don't want any of this meat," Marcel replied. "Not after El Chupacabra has gotten to it."

Marcel looked noticeably shaken and continued. "The police are now involved, Gringo. They don't believe either. They are suspecting us – the workers! We are now being made to stand watch at night to protect the livestock. I don't want to be out after dark, Gringo, but if we don't catch El Chupacabra, the police are going to start arresting us. We may get deported! Gringo, these are bad times my friend."

"Have you seen this Chupa-whatever with your own eyes?" Bobby asked.

"Yes," Marcel replied. "Once. About a year ago. I was out processing the milk and Mr. Franks asked if I could work late as he needed help putting up the hay. Mr. Franks is a good boss, a hard man, but the pay is good. I agreed.

"It was a very hot summer day and Mr. Franks suggested that the hay be put up in the evening when things cooled down. I was out in the field and had just finished loading the last bale of hay on the wagon when I spotted something over on the far ridge.

"I was not thinking of El Chupacabra at the time, mind you, but wanted to see if one of the cows had gotten loose.

"Mr. Franks was driving the wagon that night and left me alone to check on the animal. It was some distance away, but when I got there I could not believe my eyes!

"It had the body of a small man – possibly a boy – however its eyes were aglow. It had just killed an animal, but it wasn't one of our cows. It was a small cervatillo – how do you say, a fawn. It had pinned the animal on the ground and was crouched over, drinking blood from its neck!

"It looked directly at me with hate-filled eyes, but continued eating. I almost could not move, but I ran back to barn to let Mr. Franks and the other farmers know what I saw.

123

"They all laughed at me. When I brought them back to show them, El Chupacabra was gone and so was the fawn."

"I bet you were the laughing stock of the town that night," Bobby said, scoffing Marcel.

"Let them laugh," Marcel replied. "I know what I saw that night. El Chupacabra is here Bobby! None of the farms are safe."

That conversation took place about three months ago. But each evening afterwards, Bobby Luellan would roam around the countryside between Wolf Summit and Melas not trying to catch a glimpse of Marcel's mysterious vampire, per say, but looking for dead animals that he could eat.

"Damn fool," Bobby commented out loud about his friend. "His brain was probably cooked in the summer heat. Ain't no Chupabooba out here. Probably some coyote, that's all."

Then, one autumn night while trespassing on a farmer's property, he discovered the bodies of several goats that had been killed. He thought he had hit the jackpot. One by one, he began carrying them off and back to his little trailer. The task took him most of the night, but when he was done, he had collected five animals.

As dawn approached, he realized he was very hungry. He pulled out his trusty Buck knife and gutted one of the goats. He was very grateful that the animal had been bled, as that made it less messy for him. He sat on his porch and ate the flesh and organs of the goat, leaving only its skin and bones.

Half-delirious, he realized the night's activities had left him very tired. It was time for a rest and Bobby staggered into his bed.

Later that same morning, began the first of Bobby Luellan's bizarre dreams.

He dreamed that he was in a Nazi concentration camp and tied to a pole. It was back in World War II. Bobby was nowhere near old enough to have been alive during that time, but nevertheless, he was there in his mind.

"We've got a live one here, Commander," one of the Nazi soldiers said as he kicked Bobby in the side. "Caught him stealing rations, we did."

The 'Commander' leaned up close to take a look at Bobby.

"Is he retarded?" the Commander asked the soldier.

"Speak to the Commander!" the soldier instructed. The soldier spoke in German, but Bobby heard it in English – it was his dream after all.

Bobby looked up at the Commander who was the spitting image of Heinrich Himmler with a rounded face, short hair, wire-rimmed glasses, and a thin mustache.

"I, uh, didn't kill those animals," Bobby blurted out. "It was El Chupa…"

Bobby did not get to blurt out the last part of his sentence. Himmler cracked him across the face with a rod he was carrying. It left an instant mark and blood trickled down his left cheek just below his eye.

"I believe he is retarded!" Himmler then struck Bobby across the other side of the face. "There. Your injuries are even on both sides."

Bobby hunkered down and started crying. "Why are you doing this!"

"You stole the Fuhrer's meat! Those were his goats!"

"I didn't steal no goats!" Bobby moaned. "They were dead. El, El, El," Bobby began a stuttering fit.

Himmler placed a boot on Bobby's chest. "We may have to chop off your hands for your crime!"

Bobby screamed.

When he opened his eyes, he was back in his trailer. His mother and a policeman stood over him.

"The boy needs help, Mrs. Luellan."

"Please Officer McCoy," Mrs. Luellan begged. "Don't take him to jail."

"That's up for the magistrate to decide. But I will recommend a psychological evaluation be performed to see if he is a danger to himself or others."

"Get up boy, let's go!" Todd McCoy commanded, as he lifted Bobby up by his shoulder.

Bobby Luellan was only vaguely aware as he was escorted through the trailer that he had hung the carcasses of the goats from the living room ceilings. The entrails of the animals spilled out from each of them on the floor just below, gore seeping into the carpet below. The newly-saturated flooring squished underfoot as they walked through, leaving shoeprints where they stepped.

126

Bobby's mother wept horribly as the two left the trailer. Bobby had always been a slow one, but she could not even begin to fathom what she came home to this morning.

She worked as a night-shift waitress over at the Tarklin Roadside Café. When she got off her shift, she found Bobby passed out over one pile of entrails. Each of the five goats had been hung by their necks to hooks Bobby had screwed into the ceiling. It was an obscenely gory sight.

As the police cruiser pulled away, Mrs. Luellan screamed.

CHAPTER 12

The snow had started to ease off as the F-150 pulled into the small carport adjacent to Jonathan's trailer. William had been watching out the window for the two to arrive and was quick to open the door.

"Mandy!" he hollered as he ran out into the snow and gave his aunt a big hug.

"Willie!" she said in gleeful reply. "Jeez, you're all grown up." Amanda smiled and turned to Jonathan, "The last time I saw Willie, he was a little squirt!" She made a gesture with her hand about three feet off the ground.

William, who was now in his teens and much taller, smiled at the comparison.

"Let's go inside folks, it's freezing out here!" Jonathan remarked.

Inside the humble trailer, William had already set the table and some containers of take-out Chinese food was neatly arranged for them to partake in.

Over dinner, Amanda and William caught up on old times. Jonathan learned that Amanda used to babysit for William when he was a toddler and it was only when Amanda was in her teens and 'went away' that they stopped seeing each other. That was around the same time that William's life began to fall apart as well. In some eerie coincidence these two were both from fucked-up families who independently overcame adversity to make a better life on their own.

Jonathan was only half paying attention to their conversation when William made an interesting remark. "So Mandy, how did things work out between you and Stan O'Donnel?"

"We broke it off about a year ago," Amanda replied. She looked at Jonathan, "We were high school sweethearts.

"I should have broken it off a long time before," she reflected. "When I was in the hospital, he never came to visit. After I got out, we started seeing each other again."

Amanda looked into her now-cold coffee and said, "He became Sherriff of Harrison County after that Jackson fellow was injured."

Jonathan felt the first chill begin to creep over him and feared where this conversation was heading. He knew James Jackson all right. In fact, he was on Jackson's shit list of suspects in some of the weird things going on in Melas – his home town. To this day, Jonathan did not know if he was still being investigated by Jackson, but if he could avoid him, he would.

Yes, the night he met James Jackson was the night Lucy died. It took Jonathan a long time to get over Lucy and even to this day, he never took for granted how quickly life could take a turn for the worse; how quickly someone you love could be taken from you.

For a moment in memory, Jonathan was taken back to that terrible night – the night he realized that vampires were not some figment of imagination but very real. The night he realized that real vampires were not some sparkling hunk boys, but ruthless demons from hell sent to rape, kill, and destroy. To devour life – to consume if for their own selfish gain.

Jonathan did not realize that a tiny tear had streamed down his cheek as he thought back to that evening.

Lucy worked at the Melas Industrial Home For Troubled Youth, the state-ran institution where William McConnellson, III – who was sitting directly across from him now at the table – was incarcerated in.

Lucy and Jonathan had only been seeing each other for a few days, but it was love at first site. When she wasn't working, they were hanging out and dreaming of a future together.

That fateful night, Lucy and Jonathan were making out under the stars when she got an emergency call from her boss and needed to report to work right away. One of the students (inmates) had been found murdered on the property and all of the staff was being brought in to handle the traumatized juveniles.

Jonathan brought Lucy to work that night and dropped her off at the entrance to the center. As she walked inside, James Jackson stopped Jonathan and began questioning him in the boy's murder as well as wondering about another boy who had gone missing that very night!

Jonathan didn't know what the hell was going on and although he had nothing to do with either of the separate crimes, Jackson led him to believe that he – Johnny – was a suspect being that he had just recently shown back up in town after a long time of being away.

A second tear streamed down his face before Amanda and William broke their conversation and noticed Jonathan's distress.

"What's the matter, honey?" Amanda asked.

"It's the Industrial Home, isn't it?" William affirmed, knowingly.

Amanda seemed confused. Somebody at this table had to bring her up to speed. Unfortunately, neither of the hosts were talking.

"I am sorry to ruin everyone's dinner," Jonathan said. He stood up. "If you'll excuse me, I need to freshen up. I'll be right back."

When the two were alone, it was William who broke the awkward silence. "Jonathan rescued me from the school that night."

"He did what?" Amanda asked in astonishment. "I thought everyone was killed in the explosion. I had no idea that you were still in there! Oh my God, Willie." She reached across the table and hugged her nephew tightly.

William decided to reveal the terrors of that night to his aunt, for better or worse. "That's not all. Jonathan's girlfriend was killed that night. I watched it happen with my own eyes."

131

Amanda studied William's expression as he added, "She was raped before she was murdered."

"What?" Amanda said, not able to comprehend what William was saying. "I thought the explosion, fire, whatever killed those people. I am really confused."

"A murderous monster – a vampire – attacked the school that night. All of the students and staff were gathered in the cafeteria. It got in there somehow and began killing everyone.

"I had not gone in with the others and was hiding in the bathroom. Once I heard the commotion, I watched the crimes unfold on the security cameras in the principal's office."

This time it was William's turn to cry, "Mandy, I saw it all. The vampire killed them ALL! He killed them all."

She hugged him tightly and he sobbed in her shoulder.

He pulled away to finish the tale, "When all of the others had finally died, the vampire and I were the only two left in the building." A look of sheer determination came over his face. "I torched the place, Mandy."

Amanda was trying to put the pieces together, "And Johnny?"

"Jonathan – Johnny – was out in the parking lot and saw the school go up. I yelled for him to rescue me and he did."

"Did you go to the police?" Amanda asked.

"No, we couldn't. Hell Mandy, there was a vampire loose in the school! Nobody would believe me. Besides, I was a juvey boy. Do you think they would have bothered listening to me? They would have locked me up and thrown away the key. If it wasn't for Jonathan, my life would have been ruined."

"So, you came up to Canada after that?" Amanda asked.

"More or less. We did go back." William replied.

"You went back?" Amanda asked.

"To dispense justice," William replied. "There were three vampires besides the one that attacked the school. It had been a couple years since the night of the school fire and when we came back, the town was decimated. The vampires had either killed or drove off the townsfolk. Melas was a ghost town."

William starred out blankly towards the wall, "The sad thing is, nobody will ever believe us." He looked back at his aunt. "But that's the truth."

"This is creepy, but it's starting to make sense," Amanda said.

William raised a questioning eyebrow.

"Stan – my ex – and his partner Todd McCoy became obsessed with a case about two years ago." Amanda said. "In fact, it was right around the time of the school fire, when that Jackson fellow got hurt.

"Animals all around started dying. The strange thing was they were all found drained of blood.

"At first, Stan thought it was some kids pranking local farmers. But later, he thought there might be some deranged lunatic out there thinking he was a vampire."

Amanda shuddered and continued, "It got bad for us. He started spending days and nights with his buddy Todd. In fact, I thought they were homos for each other because he showed no interest in me. Whenever we would go out, all he ever talked about was the case. After a while, he started insisting that Todd go with us on dates to discuss their progress." She grimaced, obviously upset at the recollection. "You know where we'd go on date night?"

William shrugged.

"We'd drive around Melas! Of all fucking places, Willie, he'd take me to that creepy ghost town. Stan kept saying that if we patrolled long enough, we'd catch the perpetrator.

"It finally weirded me out and I had to break it off with him. Funny thing is, right before coming up here, I saw in the newspaper that a young boy matching Ralphie Edwards description was seen roaming round the graves near the city. Do you know him?"

"I can't say that I do, Mandy," William replied.

"Ralphie was one of the boys that disappeared that same night the school blew up. He was thought to have died, most people think he did."

William became noticeably pale.

Amanda said what William had feared, "I personally thought differently. I thought Stan's blood sucking lunatic was not some crazed person after all, but a real vampire. A vampire named Ralphie Edwards!"

"Holy fucking shit," William exclaimed, momentarily forgetting his recent Catholic teachings to control his temperament and tongue.

"What's wrong, Willie?" Amanda asked.

"If what you say is true," William replied, "then we did not get all the vampires in Melas when we returned to take care of Victor Rothenstein and his seethe." He pounded his fists on the table. "No, no, no!"

Jonathan, who had returned early enough to hear Amanda's recount of the new menace, placed a comforting hand on William's shoulder. "Please William," Jonathan said. "Try to calm down. We'll figure something out."

The three of them moved their conversation from the small kitchen table to the living room couches where they talked at length on whether or not to return to Melas.

"Honestly, I say we let bygones be bygones," Jonathan said. "We have a pretty good gig here – in spite of the bad weather – and hopefully, things will work itself out."

"You really think that?" William asked. "I can't possibly see how you can sit there, knowing they're still out there!"

"I agree with you, Will," Jonathan replied. "Someone needs to put a stop to it, or them. Hell, I don't know if that Edwards boy is the last of them. I thought we got them all last time we were down there."

"We have to go back!" William protested. "If we don't, Alex would have died in vain."

Jonathan grimaced. William did have a point. Had it not been for the courage of Alexander Van Helsing, they would not have been nearly as successful in defeating the three ruthless vampires during their last trip. Then there was that thing with the obelisk. Alex was obsessed that they destroy that first before taking on Victor Rothenstein in the Madison House.

Jonathan slumped back into the couch. "I'm not really sure what to do."

"I have an idea." It was Amanda. "As much as I didn't like how this case changed Stan, he told me privately that he thought that if they didn't find some sicko, they might actually find that a vampire was behind all this."

Amanda shook her head remorsefully. "Truth was, I didn't believe him about the vampire bit and that was when I started backing out of the relationship. I really thought he had started to lose it – that the case had finally cracked his sanity. I don't really regret that we broke up because his lifestyle and mine are quite different. However, if anyone could help us, it would be him.

Jonathan carefully considered the consequences of going back to West Virginia. "You do realize that going to the police opens a really big can of worms for us, don't you Amanda?"

She put her arm around him, "I do, honey. I do. In fact, if you and Willy want to stay up here, I'll keep your secret and not mention a thing of it to Stan. We haven't spoken in a good while anyway." She paused then added, "But to tell you the truth, I'm sorta scared going back if there really are bloodthirsty vampires on the loose."

"Suppose you call him and we leave out the school part," William proposed, thinking of how to skirt around the issue that he was both an escapee of a juvenile detention center as well as an arsonist. Maybe saving West Virginia wasn't such a hot idea after all.

"Well, if we stay as the Lake Family," Jonathan proposed, finally coming around to the idea, "then we could say that we were on vacation last summer with Father Van Helsing when our car – his Explorer – got smashed. We'll say the accelerator got stuck and we ran off the road, striking that granite monument."

"The obelisk," William corrected.

"Yeah. So afterward, we went up to the old Madison House to get help and were attacked. They killed Van Helsing and we killed them. We fled – being Canadian, after all – and never said a word to anyone."

"Not a bad cover if I do say so myself, William replied.

"Mandy," William asked, "what's going to be your story to you ex-boyfriend when he asks how you are associated with us?"

"I'll just tell him that we met on the Net," she said this in a loving way and hugged Jonathan tightly and laughed. "And when I learned that you guys knew something about the vampires of Melas, I had to let Stan know about it."

"Sounds like a plan," William said.

"The plans of the damned," Jonathan said grimly.

"The best laid schemes of mice and men go oft awry, as the poet, Robert Burns, would put it, but I have a good feeling about this," Amanda soothed.

"Let's hope you're right." Jonathan added. "God I hope so."

***

A sleepy-sounding Stan O'Donnel answered the phone. "Hello."

"Hey Stan, it's me."

"Mandy? How the hell have you been?"

"Okay, I guess. I may have some information on the vampire case."

"I'm all ears, babe. But before you spill the beans, I want to tell you Todd arrested some boy this morning."

"You don't say?" Amanda asked questioningly. "And in the *morning*?"

"Yep. Some retard named Luellan."

"A girl."

"No. That's his last name. Robert Luellan. Seventeen. Very slow dude who likes to eat roadkill."

"That's disgusting! And you're thinking this mentally-challenged boy is your serial animal killer?"

Stan seemed to sense where Amanda was going with that logic, "Well, between you and me toots, I'm not completely sure. But it *is* a lead.

138

"Todd found the nutjob in his house with five goats. All of them had been drained of their blood and were hanging from the living room ceiling of his mother's trailer. Are you hearing me, Mandy? The living room ceiling for crying out loud!"

"Shit!" Amanda replied. "That does sound kind of crazy."

"You ain't kidding. Todd got a lead a while back about this Luellan fellow. Some folks saw him eating road kill out along the highway near his home.

"Every morning, Todd would make it a point to drive by the Luellan household looking for anything suspicious. Today, he got the break he needed."

"He did?" Amanda asked.

"Yep." Stan replied. "Todd saw a goat's leg – mostly gnawed off – in the boy's front yard, along with some entrails on the porch.

"Of course, Officer McCoy didn't know they were goat parts at the time, but had enough probable cause to enter the Luellan residence.

"Luellan was on the living room floor screaming about Nazis or some crazy shit.

"His mother works nights and when she came home, she flipped out. It's going to take a lot of money to fix up that trailer. He trashed it with the animal parts. It looks more like a butcher shop then a residence."

"Well," Amanda replied. "My news may not matter, but I have someone who says that a real vampire may be the culprit of the animal killings."

"You don't say?" Stan replied. "Mandy, aren't you the one who thought I was crazy when I told you I suspected a vampire was involved?"

"Yes, Stan, I did. And I hope you see that I am swallowing my pride coming to you about the lead."

"Well, you do have a point," Stan mused. "Tell me what you got."

Amanda went on to describe the revised version of Jonathan and William's story, including the details of how Victor Rothenstein burst into flames when he was killed and set the Madison House on fire.

"Babe, that's a pretty incredible story," Stan replied after she was finished. "I don't know whether to believe you or consider you as crazy as that Luellan fellow is."

"You son-of-a-bitch," Amanda replied coarsely, "I'm telling you the truth. Besides I'm a sex addict and road kill is not my thing, so there!"

Stan and Amanda both laughed.

"Okay," Stan replied. "If what you say is true, then we need you and the Lakes to come downtown and get a statement. If you can do it tonight, that would be great because Todd's taking the Luellan kid down to Weston to see if they can get a psychiatric evaluation ordered up.

"With Christmas being only two days away and all, his mother is fighting tooth and nail to keep him home. Shit, I don't blame her. If I was his parent, I'd want his ass home to clean up the mess. I'd knock him simple if he were my son!"

"That may be a little bit easier said than done, Stan." Amanda said. "I'm up near Toronto on vacation."

"Shit, Mandy," Stan replied. "Whatcha doing up there?"

Amanda proceeded to explain to Stan about meeting Jonathan on the Internet and how they were spending time together taking in Christmas lights. Stan wasn't completely happy with that, but being that he and Amanda were no longer seeing each other, didn't have a real dog in the fight.

He did, however, worry that they had arrested the wrong man and if so, the real killer was still out there.

"Can I call you back in a few minutes?" Stan asked.

"Sure, you have my cell."

"By the way, you said you were vacationing near Toronto. Where exactly?"

"I'm in a little town called Colefax. Sunnycroft Trailer Court, if you must know."

"Just curious is all. I'll talk to you soon." With that, he hung up.

***

Stan O'Donnel headed back to the evidence room and pulled the file on the Madison House. Reading through the State Fire Marshall's report, he learned that indeed this house was thought to be the epicenter of a fire that had destroyed half the town of Melas and nearly one hundred acres of pristine forest in the surrounding area.

"My God!" Stan exclaimed to himself as he read the report. At the very least, he would like to get John and Will Lake in for questioning about the fire. And to think his ex-girlfriend was hanging out with them!

The next thing in the file made his blood run cold. It was the Coroner's Report. In it, he learned the forensic team had found the remains of Jennifer Abraham and Lucy Westerna. Both bodies were burned beyond standard recognition and DNA was required to identify the remains.

"What the fuck?" Stan said. One of the few things left of Ms Abraham's remains was her teeth. On a photograph attached to the report were a pair of blackened teeth, charred from the fire. Although they were black, Stan knew beyond any doubt that those were no ordinary teeth. They were fangs.

***

Within two hours, the Royal Canadian Mounted Police were at the trailer of Jonathan and William Lake. Stan O'Donnel requested that the party be immediately escorted to the Toronto International Airport and flown down to Clarksburg, West Virginia, USA.

He advised the authorities that the group was not being arrested, but were needed for a late-breaking development in a two-year old serial killer case. "These folks are key witnesses," he had told them, "and their presence could not wait until after the Christmas holiday."

Now, all that Stan could do was to wait. Wait for them to come down and sort everything out. That, or throw all their asses in jail.

He couldn't take a chance that the real killer (or should he say *killers*) were Jonathan and William Lake and not Bobby Luellan after all. He also couldn't shake the eerie feeling that the real evil was still out there and that someone else had fangs just like Mrs. Abraham's.

***

"I wonder what will happen to my Porsche," Amanda reflected from her seat aboard a redeye flight 25,000 feet above the earth.

"This whole thing is a bit awkward, if you ask me," Jonathan remarked.

The three of them had been abruptly escorted right out of the trailer and to the airport, carrying only the clothes on their backs and no carry on luggage. Several of the trailer park residents gathered outside their trailers in the snow to watch the police car whisk the three away.

It was more of a spectacle than any real criminal threat, but Jonathan couldn't help but think he would have to be moving soon if he did wind up getting out of this current predicament. The neighbors would be talking and that was the last thing Jonathan Harker (a.k.a. Jonathan Lake) needed at the moment.

Jonathan leaned over and whispered in Amanda's ear: "I think I should have stayed in your hotel room sweetheart. Had we stayed in bed, your Porsche would have been safe and sound."

"Yeah," Amanda said regrettably. "Now it will probably be towed."

A few seats down, William slept. Both could hear him snoring.

"At least he can sleep," Jonathan remarked.

"Hey baby, follow me," Amanda said, getting up from her seat. "I may have just the cure for your insomnia."

The two lovebirds headed for the bathroom to become the latest members of the Mile High Club.

CHAPTER 13

As dawn made its way across the sleepy hills near Melas on December 24th, the nightmare in the dark raged on underneath its darkened hollows.

A ragged-grey figure, hardly human, but the size of a man, wrestled on the mine floor with Kevin, giving unearthly shrieks. The others had hardly recovered from their ordeal and stood frozen in shock, but Jeff, his small pick still in his hand, swung it over his head and into the bony back of the creature pinning down his boss. The piercing point caught in the dank cloth of its shirt and bit through the flesh beneath, but no blood appeared. The coal pick stuck in the creature's back.

Tom lunged forward to pull off the beast that was nattering its teeth around Kevin's head. Jeff held the shaft of the pick and set one foot on the creature's back to gain purchase. He tugged and wriggled out the pick and struck again, but the small metal pick appeared to do little to deter the beast. As if no more irritated than by a child tugging at its shirttails, it turned its matted, grizzled head towards Jeff, and the men gasped at the sight before them.

Sightless eyes, as if veiled by thick cataracts, appeared to gaze soullessly from a grey-green face. What was worse was the mask of rich crimson blood that heavily covered the lower half of its face, its nose and cheeks dripping with Kevin's life-blood, and its gaping maws – chewing lewdly and open-mouthed on gobbets of his flesh with razor-sharp teeth.

Kevin lay with his throat ripped open, veins, muscles and tendons exposed, bubbles of blood foaming up from the ragged gash as he struggled to breathe.

"Oh, fuck!" cried Tom, and almost lost his grip.

With a mighty 'thwack,' Bubba kicked the creature's head with his massive boot, and sent its scrawny body reeling like a crow hit at speed by an SUV. It flapped and spun and crumpled. In one swift movement, Bubba picked up the creature and hurled its body like a pile of rags into the chasm below them. A sickening howl emitted from the creature until a distant crack silenced it below.

By the time Bubba turned around, Jeff was kneeling over Kevin, his hands pressed against his throat, attempting to staunch the flow. Kevin struggled to speak, much against their pleading for him to lie still.

"Some... wind!" he smiled, and breathed his last, his eyes dimming before them as his spirit left.

Jeff – having felt the pulse waver and stop – lifted his blood-drenched hands from Kevin's throat. Trembling, Jeff proceeded to close his boss's eyelids to cover over Kevin's staring, dead eyes, leaving more smears of blood like macabre finger-paintings on the man's ravaged face.

"Holy fucking shit!" began Tom, his teeth chattering, "What the hell was that?"

Neither Jeff nor Bubba could answer. Jeff merely stared down at his blood-slicked hands, and shook his head slowly. All three sat on the mine floor and recovered their breath, struggling to come to terms with what had happened, and lost in their own thoughts momentarily.

Bubba muttered, "Was it - an old miner? A homeless guy, gone mad? Was that even human?"

"Kinda. Maybe... Once," shrugged Jeff.

"Some kind of ghoul?"

They sat in silence for a moment, contemplating impossibilities. Eventually, Tom spoke, clapping his hand on Bubba's knee, "Good job, Bubba, lad. At least we've got rid of it."

"Thing is - are there more of them?" asked Jeff.

A howl, high above the sound of the rushing water, accompanied by another deeper, guttural moan, gave them their answer. The sounds came from somewhere deep within the shaft of Runner's Ridge - the Howling Shaft indeed. All three looked quickly from one to the other, wide-eyed in fear.

"Oh, Jesus, Mary and Joseph!" cried Bubba, and looked close to tears.

Tom stood up, determined, "'Let's get the hell out of here!"

"But which way?" asked Jeff, genuinely at a loss, "Kevin was the one who'd read the map. Forward into the Howling Shaft? Or back?"

"N…na…na-nah," stammered Bubba, "I can't go back that way again." He held out his hands, which were shaking uncontrollably.

"He's right, though," said Tom, "We need to go on ahead if we stand any chance of getting out of here… alive."

"Okay, let's get ready to go," Jeff gently removed Kevin's dislodged hard hat and switched off its lamp. He unscrewed the fastening and pocketed the head torch. Then he took the hand pick from Kevin's belt, explaining, "Kevin won't need these now, but we might."

Tom bit his lip, looking down at his old colleague with regret. He'd had many run-ins with Kevin, but all in the spirit of camaraderie in the end. Surely Kevin had got used to his brusque and direct Scottish ways? One of the last things he'd said to Kevin was 'Go to Hell.' He had meant no malice, but Tom couldn't help wondering if he had actually cursed him there. Or was Kevin the one who had been blessedly released? Were they the ones who were now in Hell?

Bubba, following Jeff's lead, scouted for another weapon. He picked up a hefty rock and put it in his pocket. He gripped his pick in his fist, white-knuckled, and ready for all comers.

Warily, they trudged along the walkway to the other side of the ravine, their eyes sweeping across the darkness from the wide ledge they stood on, across the lip of the abyss, to above their heads at the rocky heights above. Jeff marveled at the rich seams of coal still in evidence, and yet the shaft had long fallen into disuse. Okay, so it had been declared dangerous and unsafe, but that had never stopped greedy mine-owners before? Or even those who wished to invest in the mine to generate further income?

Speculate to accumulate. As an ex-banker, Jeff would live by this tenet. He couldn't see the sense in leaving vast seams of high quality coal untouched, while working poorer areas – where seams were so narrow that industrial equipment was inappropriate – and men were forced to pick at the coal. It was ridiculous and made no economic sense. They would have been able to shore up the shafts, rebuild the bridges and walkways, surely? Unless... there were other reasons to close up this part of the mine.

The water rushed some distance beneath them, but at least they were on the other side from the deluge racing over the drop-off, which now flowed relentlessly from the entrance they had come through, and into the depths below. They were still above the river level, but they would need to traverse deeper if Kevin's hunch was right. Either by manufactured shaft or natural hole, they needed to get out of that place, and fast.

The sound of the coursing water beneath them drowned out an eerie skittering noise two hundred yards behind them, back where Kevin had been attacked. A dark, bestial figure clattered its claw-like fingernails against the rocky walls, its long grey hair swinging in greasy ropes, as it scrambled down a fissure in the coal seam towards Kevin's bloody body.

***

"Here's the opening to the secondary shaft. It's a drift - a working off the main shaft," Tom said, unnecessarily, feeling a need to break the silence.

The enclosed space was blacker still than the darkness they had left, and the roof was little higher than Bubba's head. Indeed, Bubba's bulk almost filled the width too. The three men entered the narrow shaft, oblivious to the danger behind them.

CHAPTER 14

The obelisk once again shined a dark, vivid green. Not a single snowflake marred its shinny, yet porous surface.

"They have awoken," came Legion's voice through Ralphie.

"Indeed they have," replied Talman.

"Where is your brother?"

"Don't worry, I will let him know. He will be ready. He has positioned himself in the ideal spot for The Plan to come together."

Ralphie, Talman, and Legion communed and began chanting arcane incantations known only to the necromancer Talman and the demon.

The sounds of wails and moaning could be heard as if the very ground itself was in trauma.

In a rare showing of disobedience to his possessor, Ralphie's old self broke the chant. "I don't like this, I want it to stop."

"What you like does not matter anymore," Talman replied. "Only the Master's will is what matters."

"Yes, I have been a willing vessel for my Master, but I was told that I would see my mommy again and I haven't. You lied!"

Talman looked confused, as he was not privy to the original deal struck between Legion and the boy.

Suddenly, Legion began speaking through Ralphie. The two began a conversation within the same body of the nine-year-old boy that looked quite disturbing to Talman as he watched it unfold.

"The deal will still be honored."

"It's been two years!"

"All in due time."

"I'm tired of waiting."

"You will wait, you have no choice."

"You promised, God damn you. You promised!"

Ralphie's body flew through the air and struck the obelisk and fell to the ground. The aurora of Legion momentarily stepped clear of the boy and faced him as a ghost-like apparition. Ralphie trembled at the site of the manifestation.

"All in due time. I promise you that before this very day ends, you will see her. But, alas, the dawn approaches!"

The spirit jumped back into Ralphie's body and stood up. "We must be off."

Talman stood quietly by the obelisk and watched the sunrise alone.

CHAPTER 15

Back in the darkness where Kevin lay dead, even before the dark and awful scrambling creature had reached Kevin's body, a second hunched creature emerged from the darkness in another direction, clambering forward. Then another, and another, until a dozen dead-eyed ghouls came swarming up from the edge of the chasm and out of rocky cracks like massive roaches, and fell upon Kevin's corpse with sinister hisses and shrieks.

They joined together and became a black mass of writhing bodies; rags, hair and grey bony limbs that elbowed one another, jostling for space, ferreting into the body. They tore at Kevin's clothes with their claws, ripping his skin with jagged teeth, sinking their fangs into exposed skin, sucking thirstily at raw flesh. Where Kevin's blood had gushed and pooled before he died, creatures lapped at the bloody puddles with long grey tongues, shoving each other out of the way, snorting and snuffling like hogs, pressing cold lips to the stained ground to suck up every drop.

They feasted rabidly upon the corpse and only stopped when Kevin was nothing more than a ragged red mess of blubber and bone, staining the ground.

A single body, with fewer than seven pints of blood already soaked into the parched earth, was not enough to satisfy the primal needs of twelve undead who had not eaten or drunk for years. Worse still, a taste of blood had literally given them a taste for blood. Mindlessly, they had lived in this hinterland, this midway world between life and death, not human nor vampire. They had no memory, no thinking skills at all, just a burning hunger - an animal lust for blood.

Deprived of this driving need since the day each of them had been killed, this was their first taste of their true purpose. And they were not satiated by the remains of one dead man already sucked dry by his ragged killer and by the dusty, absorbent ground where he lay. One ghoul, vaguely female in form, raised her nose in the air, nostrils flaring obscenely, and snuffled greedily as if catching a scent on a breeze.

Murmuring incoherently, one-by-one they raised their ugly, ashen heads and sniffed the air with bloodied snouts. First one, then another stood up slowly and turned their veiled eyes towards the distant shaft opening. In the same direction that Jeff, Bubba, and Tom had taken just twenty minutes before.

***

A mile or so further on, Tom led the way through the depths of the narrow drift, which steadily angled downwards. He was alert to the underlying dangers of deserted mines. False floors were often apparent in any lengths of tunnel, where the floor level has been worked and underscored.

These floors might only be supported by rotten wood. However, they were faced with a layer of rock, looking like a solid floor.

Also, the ventilation and water pumping systems that made for safe working conditions would have been removed when the mine was abandoned and capped off. Bad air was always a concern in any mine, worse still in a disused one.

Tom was ever cautious of the potential of finding bad air. Old mine workings were particularly hazardous, owing to pockets of blackdamp - stagnant air with low levels of oxygen. Tom had lost his calibrated 4-gas detector in the mine car, so he had neither a prior warning device nor technical awareness of the existence of high concentrations of methane, carbon monoxide, carbon dioxide or hydrogen sulfide. Coal mines were especially prone to releasing these gases. Each of these could either displace the oxygen in the narrow tunnel, suffocating them where they stood; poison them outright, or cause an explosion.

Unfortunately, there was no time given their present predicament to deliver a lecture on these hazards. Tom was aware that the oxygen was thinning, and soon they would begin to choke. He hurried through ahead of the others, hoping that they would find some ventilation soon.

At the back of the trio, Bubba traced his hands against the walls on each side of the drift, turning his head uneasily around, the beam of his lamp picking up the uneven wall and ceiling of rock and the wooden supports bracing up the tunnel along the way. He hadn't wanted to be last through the drift, yet here he was, bringing up the rear and feeling vulnerable. But he hadn't wanted to be first either, that was for sure. So Tom had taken the lead.

Bubba glanced over his shoulder every few steps. What if that thing had survived? What if it were climbing up the steep sides of the underground ravine coming to get them? He turned around, and walked a few steps backwards, but that was unsustainable. The drift inclined gently downwards and underfoot was rocky and uneven, making him move slowly so that he lost pace with the others and pitched sideways into the wall, scraping his elbows.

That was the least of his worries, he knew, and falling over on his back like a helpless beetle was not in his itinerary. Moreover, he couldn't see Jeff in front of him unless he faced forward, and he needed to know that he wasn't alone. He turned to face the way they were walking again, keen to keep up, treading on Jeff's heels if that's what it took to keep close by. The hairs on the back of his neck prickled up, and he still glanced over his shoulder from time to time, paranoid.

Although the three had maintained a tense silence since they entered the drift, Jeff was aware of Bubba's labored breathing behind him, heating up his own sweating neck, too close for normal comfort. As if the environment wasn't claustrophobic enough, the walls, floor and ceiling closing in upon them, there was

Bubba using up more than his share of air and smelling of fear.

Jeff understood Bubba's need. However, he resisted the urge to tell the big guy to back off a little. Especially each time his clumsy boots caught the back of Jeff's heels, as if he would have stampeded over him, given half a chance.

Jeff quickened his own pace to narrow the gap between himself and Tom, who was moving swiftly down ahead, his boots almost skipping across the debris. All the more disturbing, here was a guy in his sixties, work-hardened and admittedly uncertain of the right route.

A few yards ahead, Tom breathed in a change in the air. His lamp picked up an opening out of the drift as it widened below him. His heart raced with anticipation. A good flow of air was an encouraging sign, suggesting underground volume. All his hopes rested on this being an 'adit' - a drift with a portal leading to the outside.

His mind raced with possibilities. Better still, it could be a compartment - an area that housed a cage or a coal skip that could elevate them to the surface. Some compartments contained emergency exits - a small cage or ladders used as an escape route. At the very least it would be a ventilation shaft - a winze - or air vent, much smaller and angled underground. That would be more difficult to crawl up, and less direct, but hell - if it led to fresh air and escape, he'd take it.

But before he got his hopes up and alerted the others, he considered that this also could have been a stope, an area where the coal had been removed, and since stopes followed the vein of coal - it could have headed in any direction and at any angle - deeper beneath the surface still, and even ending blindly, trapping them completely.

Behind him, Jeff had already caught the same sight and gasped. Tom stepped down and surveyed the environment, allowing Jeff and Bubba the opportunity to step in too, and stand alongside him for the first time in a half hour. One side of chamber was bathed in a dim light from above. The air was a lot lighter, circulating fresher, and they breathed it in hungrily, delirious for oxygen.

The chamber they stood in was shored up with wooden 2x4s, holding the loose rock in place. This one resembled a large room. Stopes had a lot of loose material in them, and Tom knew to exercise extreme caution.

"Wow!" said Bubba, his relief at being out of the narrow drift obvious for all to see. He began to stumble off in the direction of the light, like a moth to a flame, but Tom held out a hand and stopped him.

"Whoah, lad!" The giant met Tom's warning gaze as the Scotsman continued, "Remember your safety briefing? Well, that counts ten times over in abandoned mines. Watch yourself. Some support structures have likely been removed for re-use someplace else, and supporting pillars could have been quarried away, leaving the chamber unstable." He stopped and gazed around, the beam of his lamp noticeably fading. "Goddamn lamp!" he cursed, rattling his hand into his tool belt and removing his helmet to replace the batteries of his head lamp.

"Looks like a raise!" he grinned.

"I can't think about money now," blustered Bubba.

"No. A raise is a six-to-twelve foot square vertical shaft, divided into two sections. Miners would use these raises to move up and down between levels of a mine," smiled Tom. "One half is a dead drop to the bottom."

He walked over to a shaft in the roof, illuminated slightly by a distant sunlight and added as an afterthought, "It's used for haulage."

Bubba and Jeff joined him and looked up at the sheer sides of the shaft. No cage, no mechanism, just the rusting framework of girders, and a vertiginous climb of several hundred feet, with no evident footholds in the rock face, and no climbing equipment. Jeff appraised their chances and determined them as slim.

Tom moved to the other side of the chamber and announced, "This other section above here is a series of platforms."

He shinned his flashlight to indicate what he was talking about. Above were platforms that were staggered about ten feet apart with holes cut in them alternately.

Tom continued, "Below each hole, usually a ladder leads to the next platform. Aha!" he clapped his hand on a moldering wooden ladder fixed to the wall.

"That's stupid. Why don't they just have one big ladder to the top?" asked Bubba.

Tom shook his head, "This construction was designed for safety: falling off a ladder meant only falling to the next platform, rather than the bottom of the entire shaft."

"I don't give a shit about falling. Just give me the quickest route out!" Bubba launched himself at the ladder, and this time, there was no stopping him. He pushed Tom aside, and was trampling up the rungs before Tom could protest, his head disappearing through the ceiling hole into the chamber above. Then his legs stopped dead, and stood rigid, three rungs from the top. His bulky waist almost filled the entrance, so Jeff and Tom could only see the lower half of his body

"Bubba!" said Tom. "What is it?"

They heard a muffled moaning sound, and Bubba's legs began to shake on the ladder rung. Tom clasped the ladder to secure it and Jeff ran to it, peering upwards.

"Bubba!"

Jeff observed that Bubba was peeing himself. First came the strong rotten vegetable smell of urine, then the darkening stain on Bubba's jeans, and the trickle of piss from beneath the worn hem and over his boots. More disturbing, was the alarming jerking of his legs, vibrating the whole fragile ladder.

Jeff clambered up behind, trying to pull Bubba down, or at the very least, see what the hell was happening, but all he could see in the gap between Bubba's belly and the entrance was darkness. All he could hear was a faint murmuring from Bubba, his body still jerking, and a strange sound like a seagull cry in the distance, like someone inhaling a whistling sound between their teeth and lips, like someone doing an exaggerated caricature of a kiss. Kissy kissy.

The jerking of Bubba's legs stopped as suddenly as the third rung from the top of the ladder cracked, and Jeff and Bubba came crashing down to the ground, a bundle of splinters and bodies, while Tom looked on in horror.

"Oh, Holy Shit!" Tom covered his mouth with his hand, and Jeff scrambled out from under Bubba's fleshy limbs to see what the hell Tom meant by that. His eyes widened in terror, mirroring the expression on what was left of Bubba's face.

Bubba lay with his eyes wide open, staring glassily up at them, his mouth wide in a mask of horror. His face was morbidly white, like marble. From one cheek to his collar-bone, a strip of skin was torn away, exposing flesh and bone; but worse still was the deep gash in his throat, pierced and shredded by something serrated, as if a hand-saw had been taken to his neck and fretted away, ripping at the flesh, beneath the suet-like layer of fat under his waxy skin. And yet, no blood. There should have been blood - arterial spray, veins flowing and gushing or dripping blood, yet there was only the slightest mark on Bubba's shirt, as if he had merely cut himself shaving. Crazy!

"What... the fuck?" muttered Jeff, before a heavy grey figure dropped through the ceiling entrance and bared its ravening teeth in a snarl. Although grey, dusty, and wild like the other creature, this one's face was more animated, and its eyes burned red, demonic. It was filled with Bubba's life-blood, and eager to feast on more, from its combative stance. It raised its claw-like arms, and Jeff recalled the trees he had seen being swept by the river flow down into the abyss, raising their arms... just like this beast. Oh... fuck. How many of them were there?

It swung its ghoulish body round, suddenly aware of Tom's presence behind it, and Jeff recovered enough to pick up a rock and take his chance. He dealt it a firm blow on the back of the head, and it gave a hideous shriek and swept round to face him. Tom unfastened his helmet and with all his might, beat it roundly about the head until it staggered and fell.

Jeff took out his coal pick and hammered it into the creature's neck, where it spurted blood. Bubba's fresh red blood, no doubt. Jeff shuddered and hacked at it again and again, splattering grey flesh, bone and sinew until its neck was a ragged stump, its head lying limp, attached only by a tatter of skin.

Jeff stood up, panting at his exertion, and he and Tom looked down on the creature, afraid it might rise again. But right before their eyes, the hideous battered grey face transformed. It became soft and delicate, and the fair-complexioned skin grew younger. The satanic red eyes changed to a cornflower blue; the features grew pretty, the hair a soft golden blonde. Before their eyes the haggard beast had become the body of a beautiful girl, all but decapitated, but certainly dead.

Jeff shuddered, and exchanged looks of shock and disbelief with Tom.

"Crap! What the fuck?"

"Let's get the hell out!" Tom began the ascent of what remained of the ladder. He heaved himself up into the ceiling hole, compensating for the missing rotted rung.

Just as Jeff stepped up the ladder to follow, he was disturbed by a wailing sound across the other side of the chamber. Pouring out of the entrance to the drift, were more ragged grey creatures, as if being spewed from Hell's mouth. He scrabbled himself up, half-dragged up by Tom, and kicked the ladder away from the wall as he went, where it smashed into rotten sticks.

The gruesome creatures gave unearthly moans, reaching their grey, stick-like arms and taloned fingers and gazing with their cataracts upwards towards the ceiling hole, just as Jeff managed to lift his feet into the platform above. His last sight of them was a sea of gruesome gnarled fingers waving and clutching at nothing, nails scratching at the air just three feet below his feet.

Scrambling to his feet with Tom's help, Jeff surveyed the scene. Another derelict platform, much like the last, but without an entrance way. The next ladder upwards was across the other side of the chamber on the opposite wall, just as Tom had said.

"Quick - that won't keep them long. Careful!" said Tom, as they ran across the platform towards the ladder.

In their terror, it was impossible for Jeff to consider that all ladders – and wooden floors in old mines especially – should be tested before trusting any body weight to them. Tom trod carefully but swiftly, his eyes on the ground, avoiding evident patches of suspicious rot. But Jeff ran like the hounds of hell were after him, and lunged with his full body weight, landing one foot with a crack on a weak area of board hidden by darkness, water, loose debris, or false floor. It splintered and gave way beneath his foot, one leg shooting down the hole in a cloud of dust and shards of rotten timber, his other leg painfully left behind on the floor level, split sideways at right angles to the other.

"Christ!" he yelled in agony, momentarily frozen in shock.

Tom made his way over to him, and commenced to put his arms under Jeff's armpits to haul him upwards.

In the platform beneath, the crashing of Jeff's limb through the ceiling had alerted the creatures. Up to that point, they had been still mindlessly swaying their arms towards the ceiling entrance that Tom and Jeff had disappeared through, just seconds before.

Then, with moans and howls, the first of the godforsaken ghouls changed their focus to Jeff's leg, its booted foot dangling. The ripped cotton of his protective suit and the denim of his jeans beneath it, were pushed up over his thigh, still left up in the space above. His leg hung down, tantalizingly, dusty, bare and bloody from a graze on his calf.

Above, Tom braced his feet against the floor joist which still seemed secure, and heaved at Jeff's armpits. Tom wrestled to get him out, but had little purchase with the rotten wood around him, and feared falling completely through. Jeff twisted his body to angle his hands towards the joist to heave himself out, but his leg remained full length through the floor.

Beneath, the creatures gathered, reaching their wizened hands upwards. One stood with its parched mouth open, jagged pointed fangs bared, and long grey tongue extended to receive the drop of blood which fell from the shallow wound on Jeff's leg. With hisses, shrieks. and jostling, the creatures scrabbled for the best position to gain access to the blood. Their hands were inches from Jeff's boot.

Jeff peered down through the shattered planks and saw how close the ghouls were. He bent up his leg in an attempt to evade their clutches, but realized that if he stood any chance of getting out the way he'd come through, he needed to extend it. He shifted his weight around, tensed his arms and placed them strong and flat against the joist, while Tom adjusted his hands again to haul out his shoulders when Jeff was prepared to heave himself upwards.

Below them, in one ghoul's mind came a vague and primitive thought. It had not needed to think for many months, and the thought process was crude and slow. But when motivated by an insatiable thirst for blood, even an undead creature with no humanity will resort to whatever it takes to attempt to satisfy its primal lust.

It jumped up. It jumped above the crowd of moaning beasts, higher than their grey, wiry heads, and grabbed at Jeff's booted foot. And held on. It scrabbled for a foothold amongst those below, and found it, tugging Jeff's foot, at the same time as raising itself towards his level, reaching its hungry mouth towards his ankle.

"Get me out!" Jeff felt the tug on his foot, braced his arms, and Tom and Jeff wrenched him upwards with all their might.

The creature had sunk its teeth into Jeff's leg, just above the boot line. He lashed out, kicking it off before he crashed back through into the platform above, leaving the creature sprawling back down below, knocking over fellow ghouls and showering the gruesome cluster of creatures in rotten wood and coal dust.

"Fuck! Ow!" Jeff scrambled up awkwardly and tested his weight on his leg. He trod a couple of times, getting the feeling back and glanced down at his scraped leg, ending with a puncture wound from the ravenous teeth of the beast below.

"You okay?" asked Tom. "Can you walk?"

"Yeah. Yeah! It's a flesh wound. Nothing!" He limped towards the ladder.

Tom stood beneath the ten foot ladder, and shook it. It seemed steady enough. "Jeff- you get up first," he said, "I can bunk you up if need be."

Jeff gratefully grabbed the ladder and mounted the first rung with his good leg, pulling up his wounded one, and stepping up to haul his weight on his best leg again.

Behind Tom, creatures were scrambling through the floor entrance, and also through the rotten hole Jeff had created. The sound of them, hissing louder now, and splintering their way through, alerted Jeff. It seemed that their recent experience with one ghoul's success in reaching higher had somehow taught them a lesson and made them collectively intelligent. They were cooperating with one another to hoist one another up. Worse still, as if attracted by the scent of fresh flowing blood, still more soulless creatures emerged from the shaft entrance and began to swarm into the room below to follow their fellow undead to the source of the blood that drove them delirious with hunger.

"Hurry!" cried Tom, pushing Jeff up. Jeff hurried as best he could, dragging his leg up into the next platform, and twisting round to help Tom up. Meanwhile, Tom was still standing at the bottom, tugging the ladder free of the wall.

"What are you doing?" shouted Jeff, reaching his hands through the opening to beckon him upwards.

"Need to pull it up behind us!" panted Tom, releasing the ladder from its rusted moorings with a creak, propping it against the opening, and stepping onto the first rung.

His delay cost him dearly. Creatures fell upon him, grabbing, pulling him from the ladder.

Jeff swung his legs over the entrance, prepared to come to his aid, "Tom! I'm coming!"

"Save yourself!" yelled Tom. "There are too many of them! Go!" He began to disappear and drown under a sea of grey writhing bodies, clamoring over him, giving sickening howls. Blood fountained up as they preyed on him, spraying the crowd, who gasped in a frenzy of delight.

Jeff pulled at the ladder, and swung it clumsily at a couple of creatures' heads, trying to fend them off Tom, but it would only delay the inevitable. Tom was right. They were hopelessly outnumbered, and Tom was already lost. Jeff's only chance of surviving was to run, and to destroy any ladders or aids along the way that would make it easy for them to follow. In fact, he needed to make barriers if anything.

He pulled up the ladder and carried it across to the entrance above. No sense in discarding a ladder that could be used in another entrance. He clambered up the secured ladder, hauled up the loose one he'd carried up from the previous platform, then kicked off the holdings and released the second ladder, pulling up that one too. This wouldn't prevent them; only delay them for a few minutes.

He looked desperately around him for anything to bar their way and saw an old rusted coal truck abandoned in the corner – a heavy barrow full of rocks and other debris. He wheeled it over the entrance hole, bracing it with the two ladders set cross-wise beneath it. Again, a deterrent rather than a permanent barrier.

He looked around wildly, and illuminated by the vertical coal shaft which gave him welcome strength in the dimming light of his head torch, he saw at last that he must be close to the surface. There were thickly coated tables and boxes, and rather than another laddered ceiling entrance, he saw an opening in the wall the other side from the main shaft. He rushed across, as fast as his throbbing leg would allow him. His throat was raw with breathing hard, his heart bursting in his chest. Meanwhile, he could still hear the cacophony of howls beneath him in the distance, driving him on.

He entered the drift, a worked passageway supported by timber trusses, and was relieved that the incline upwards was lit by a shaft of light somewhere up ahead. He breathed fresh air, felt a breeze as he faced forward, until he arrived at a wooden gateway, padlocked on the outside, where the shaft had been capped.

Kevin had told them to look out for surface shafts, where the ground around open pits and abandoned mine shafts was weak, and could cave-in without warning. If they couldn't find an open entrance or shaft, that was their only hope. Shafts could be hidden by undergrowth and timber used for capping may have rotted to a point where it could collapse with any weight. There could be an 'ant-lion trap': loose earth around a surface shaft which crumbles away over time, leaving a funnel-shaped drop-off around the shaft. But this was not an ant-lion trap, it was the main entrance to Runner's Ridge shaft, and the fresh open air was tantalizingly close.

Jeff pulled and pushed at the gate, but it was sturdy and newly replaced, designed to keep out vandals and adventurers. Wildly, he staggered around, looking for anything to lever away the gateway, back-tracking to the chamber.

Meanwhile, the howling and groaning grey creatures had swarmed up into the chamber below and were confronted by the coal truck above the entrance, blocking their way. Arms and scrawny hands lunged upwards, grabbing at the cross of ladders, swinging on the rotting wood, cracking it and pulling it away. Scrabbling on top of one another, they attempted to squeeze their emaciated bodies through the space between the truck wheels and the floor, reaching upwards and outwards. With a loud creak, the heavy truck finally fell through the rotted timbers, taking with it many grey bodies, with ear-piercing shrieks and an explosion of dust.

Jeff cast around the chamber, looking for any tool that might help, dismissing the impracticalities of tables, ropes and wooden boxes. One of the crates beneath a table was padlocked. He took out his small hand-pick, broke it open and stood back. That looked like dynamite, just three sticks. Sure enough, wiping the dust off the crate, he saw the danger symbol, and the actual word 'dynamite'. Shit. Useful, but how would he deploy it without killing himself?

Aware that dynamite and other explosive materials can become unstable over time, he carefully carried the small crate through the drift and towards the entrance gate. He left the crate a few yards down the tunnel, and took one small stick of dynamite and stood it against the dirt wall beside the gate.

Relentlessly, the first of the remaining fifteen or so ghouls clambered up over the gaping hole the coal truck had made, using its surface as a platform to enable them to haul themselves up with ease. Grown rabid with frustration, the taste of Tom's blood still on their lips, their urge for more was unstoppable. They followed the metallic scent of Jeff's leg-wound, which hung on the air, enticing them to further violence. They would not give up.

Jeff took out the spare torchlight he'd taken off Kevin's helmet, smashed the plastic cover off against the wall and switched it on, leaving the element exposed near to the dynamite. He took cover on the other side of the entrance, and threw his helmet at the spare torch to shunt it towards the dynamite. It was dangerous and foolhardy, but he had little choice remaining to him.

The blast of the explosion blew him across the overgrown driveway leading to the entrance. The shock of the first blast and the subsequent collapse of the drift set off the crate containing the rest of the dynamite. Rock, soil, coal, wood, metal and dust exploded into the air, showering Jeff's inert body where he lay, yards away. His bare leg bled slowly, the skin around the bite mark swollen and sore, as if infected.

The last thing Jeff Abraham saw before passing out was the cold December sunlight fighting for a spot against gathering storm clouds.

Lyrics from a Christmas carol came to mind as he drifted off to darkness: "Let it snow, let it snow, let it snow…"

CHAPTER 16

Back in West Virginia, after Jonathan, William, and Amanda stepped off the plane, they were ushered into a waiting police cruiser and headed for Clarksburg.

The journey was mostly silent, since they were tired and none of them really wanted to speak under the scrutiny of the two officers in the front seats. Jonathan and William looked at one another. Their close bond was such that they sometimes didn't need words, they could read one another's expressions. William looked more irritated than worried, although his young serious face held a complex mix of emotions: exhaustion, delight to be reunited with his aunt, happiness and a little jealousy that she and Johnny were getting on so well, anxiety over returning to Melas and facing the past – or worse, a present danger – and anger that their endeavors might be delayed by police inquiries.

Johnny shared many of these unspoken feelings, along with a determination to do his damnedest to clear up any mess related to their last visit. He could see that as well as having a lot of explaining to do to the police, there was evidently current vampire action that needed to be stopped as soon as possible.

If the police bought their story about the fire and let them off the hook, there would be still be some serious work to do if his instincts were right. Since they had killed off Victor Rothenstein during their last visit to this hellhole, Johnny was quietly confident that his and William's experience meant they were in a better position than the cops to deal with this. Compared to them, they were pretty well prepared to make battle with the dark forces again if need be – but could they afford to let Amanda in on the action? How would she take to becoming a 'vampire hunter' too?

Johnny glanced sideways and appraised Amanda's grimly determined face. She was a pretty hard nut, anyway. As a vampire hunter, she would probably do just fine. Then his mind wandered to more intimate things. Hmmm. She was a red hot lover, too. *So, Amanda's ex-boyfriend Stan is now the Sheriff,* Johnny pondered. Would this be an advantage to their case, or not?

At least he believes in vampires. That was a start.

Stepping into Stan's office in Clarksburg, Johnny saw Stan's immediate territorial response. He stood up lazily as if he didn't care that his ex-girlfriend and two suspects in a major criminal investigation had turned up together. He stood to his full height, stretched back his shoulders and puffed out his chest, so that his police shirt strained over his muscles. His body seemed to expand like a comic book superhero. He grazed over Amanda's body in appreciation and locked into Johnny's eyes with a steely glare. Hooking his thumbs into his belt loops, he stood and waited.

"Hi Stan!" Amanda broke the silence within a split second, spoiling the High Noon atmosphere Stan had aimed to create, and ran over to throw her arms round the Sheriff's stiff neck.

"Hey, Mand... Long time, hun."

Johnny felt an uncomfortable sensation wash over him, as he watched Stan's macho posturing melt away in Amanda's arms. Only momentarily, because the Sheriff then gave a small proprietorial smile over Amanda's shoulder to Johnny, then broke away, regaining his professional composure to turn his attention back to Johnny and William.

Johnny held out his hand, and Stan shook it, over-firmly. *He'll be arm-wrestling me for her, next!* thought Johnny, as he gripped and vigorously shook the powerful paw in return.

"Are we arrested?" piped up William, feeling left out.

"Hell, no, son," Stan ruffled William's hair, further inflaming Johnny, who felt a fatherly love for the teenage boy, and also offending Willy, who thought himself too mature to be patronized, and patted on the head like a little kid.

"Oh, Stan," cooed Amanda, turning Johnny's stomach over, as she touched Stan gently on his bare forearm, letting her fingers linger, "Can't we clear this all up?"

"I sure hope so," Stan said grimly, trying to ignore Amanda's flirtatious manner and focus on staring out Johnny.

"Please listen to their side of things, Stan."

Stan rolled his eyes, "Sure. That's what we brought you down for!"

But then Johnny looked over at Amanda, and Stan caught a softening of his expression as the new boyfriend's eyes met Mandy's. Stan was taken aback.

Well I'll be damned! The guy actually cares for her, Johnny thought.

Stan shook off sentimentality and resumed his proficient police role. "Okay, so we need statements from each of you. If you don't mind just accompanying us to the interview rooms, we'll get your stories," Stan gestured towards the door.

"It's not stories – it's the truth!" Willy retorted. They all filed out of the office, leaving Stan to follow them.

"He's a good guy, Stan," Amanda whispered as she passed him.

"We'll see," Stan responded, gruffly, determined that *he* personally was going to be the one to press this Johnny fella for information. He nodded to another officer to take William into a separate room for interview. Amanda sat nervously outside in the corridor, cradling a coffee mug in her hands.

"Interview with Johnny Lake," began Stan, for the benefit of the tape recorder, after the formalities of time, date and introductions were over. "Okay, Mr Lake, please tell me what you were doing in the time leading up to the date in question."

"We were on vacation here last summer with Father Alex Van Helsing when his Explorer was smashed in – an accident. We went up to the old

Madison House to get help and were attacked... by vampires."

"Vampires," repeated Stan. "Please can you clarify what you mean by this?"

Jonathan scowled at him, "You know – Dracula – Goth types with pointy fangs, who like drinking blood?"

"You're saying you were attacked by Goths."

"No! By vampires! Real, non-human vampires. The living dead! Look, I know it sounds crazy, but there are more things out there than we know."

"Okay, okay, but you realize this is hard to believe, huh?" Stan reached a finger towards the tape button and leant in to the microphone to say, "Sheriff Stan O'Donnel stopped the tape at 3:59 pm."

The tape clicked off, and Johnny waited, puzzled. Stan sat back and held out his palms in an expression of openness. "Look, Johnny, I don't want to make this hard for you. Truth to tell, I am inclined to believe you about these vampires. So, call me crazy as you. We even have a piece of evidence to back up your story, off the record. So, what I'm saying is, you don't have to convince me, but I want as much detail as possible, for the record. Okay?"

Johnny raised one quizzical eyebrow, as Stan pressed on the record button again. "4:01pm, interview resumed... Mr Lake, if we accept the existence of vampires, please go on with your statement of events that night."

"They attacked us and killed a priest who had been traveling with us: Father Alexander Van Helsing.

During the fight, we killed them in self defense. One of the vampires burst into flames when he died. That was what caught the house on fire. You see how crazy this all sounds. That – plus being Canadian citizens – we were scared shitless. We truly didn't know what to do if we were detained. How could we explain it? So, after barely escaping with our lives, we returned home and didn't speak of it again."

"Okay, and for the benefit of the tape, please would you explain in detail exactly what happened? Tell me everything."

Johnny took a breath and told it as it was. Incredibly, the Sheriff seemed satisfied with the story as he told it, and told them they would be free to leave. Just then, his radio blared, and he held up one finger for them to wait.

***

From the river outlets that had washed through the mines, grey ghoulish bodies lay inert in the brown river water and allowed themselves to be carried wherever they flowed by this force of nature. The heat of the mine and the force of the water had eroded the snowy edge of the riverbank, and so the river swelled above its usual levels, and grew faster. The bodies bobbed along, bumping into the bank and rocks along the way, hardly distinguishable from the icy waters, and obscured by the steadily falling snow.

Even if anyone had managed to notice these grey masses within the fast flowing waters, they might have thought them corpses, flushed out from some natural disaster. They looked like dead bodies, after all. You had to look closely to see an arm move deliberately here to push themselves off a rock, or there, to propel themselves further midstream. Little did anyone know that they were undead bodies, about to participate in an unnatural disaster.

***

Todd opened his police cruiser window to let out the reeking body odor of gore-covered Bobby Luellan, who sat in the back, blotting out the late afternoon light with his lanky, plaid-shirted body. Todd glanced at Bobby's blank, pale, moon face in the rear-view mirror.

"Okay, Bobby?"

"Uh-huh," Bobby nodded, mildly, gazing out of the window.

Todd shook his head. Dang! This childlike teenage idiot must be the animal killer, surely. The sooner they could close this case the better. Todd pressed gently on the accelerator as he drove towards Weston State Lunatic Asylum for Bobby's psychiatric evaluation.

Arriving at the asylum, Bobby allowed himself to be led through to the reception area, formally booked in, and taken into a ward. *That was pretty easy. And now my work is done!*

Todd's attention was already turning to the holidays. As if the Christmas lights and tree in the hallway weren't enough, the receptionist was wearing

178

garish tinsel earrings with flashing lights, and on her head was a green and red floppy pointed 'Santa's little helper' hat with a pompom on the end.

"Are you dyslexic? Shouldn't that be 'Satan's little helper', Mary-Lou?" smiled Todd. He'd known Mary-Lou since they were in high school, and knew she could take a teasing.

"To-odd," she scolded.

"Okay, so they'll let us know the results of the evaluation soon?" Todd asked, eager to be on his way.

"Yeah, but with it being Christmas Eve and all..." shrugged Mary-Lou.

"Yeah, yeah. Tell me about it. I guess everyone's too busy partying and playing Santa to bother solving this case with me!" Todd grumped, opening the front door, "Crap. And now it's started snowing!"

"Merry Christmas, Grinch... I mean, Todd!" Mary-Lou smiled as he left.

It was Christmas Eve, and even though it was still early, just past 4:00 pm. Todd had had enough of the day and wanted to get the hell out of Weston and get home to his family for the holidays.

He jumped into his cruiser and screeched off, the wheels kicking up a hailstorm of gravel and snow as he left. The snow had only just started but looked as if it would settle, so the quicker he got home the better. If he put his foot down, he should get home in plenty of time to be back home in his Lay-Zee Boy, feet up, with a bottle of Bud, ready to let the White Christmas commence.

179

Sheesh. That asylum always gave him the creeps, and the sooner he saw the back of it, the happier he would be. He glanced at its dark and looming shape, still visible in his rear-view mirror, between the swipes of the rear wiper. God's sake! If ever there was a good location for a horror movie, then Weston was...

BAM! The car hit something with great force. That loud noise and movement shocked Todd to attention and he gripped the steering wheel tight as it spun. He had hit something dark and bulky that had rushed across his path, out of the woods. The car shuddered over a body and lurched as it flew into the air. Todd struggled for control, but the car hit a tree. BAM! Todd's head flicked forward, bouncing into the vehicle's driver's side airbag as it deployed. Simultaneously, snow spattered down from the tree branches above.

"Crap!" yelled Todd, switching off the engine. He massaged his neck, slightly whiplashed, but otherwise he was okay. He stepped out of the car, blinking against the big white flakes of snow and ran back to the roadway, sickened and concerned at what he might find. The dark figure lay in the snow and his tire tracks, not moving at all.

It was a deer. *Thank God,* he thought. For a horrible moment, he'd thought it might be a person, a patient or someone. He dragged the deer carcass off the road, to ensure that there was safe passage for other drivers, shuddering with the cold and distaste at the large blood stain he'd left in the snow, then went back to the cruiser.

He inspected the front of the car. Shit. The front axle was broken. One wheel lay horizontal on the ground beneath the tree that had done the damage.

"Fuck! Man! It's Christmas!" Todd groaned, his shoulders becoming frosted with the driving snow.

He sat back in the car and radioed Stan to come give him a lift back to the station and take a look at the damage. He warned him it looked expensive.

Stan was still with Johnny, Amanda, and William when Todd's call came in.

"Todd! You had to choose today?" scolded Stan, "Well, to make it worth my while, I might as well bring some interesting witnesses along and kill two birds with one stone. They can fill you in on what they know, and we can see how this fits with the tooth and other evidence.

"It has an impact on Bob Luellan's freedom, if there's truth in what they say. Let's see if you agree with what my gut tells me.

"So, while you're waiting, you can make yourself useful too – see if you can hurry up that psycho test on the boy. I might as well interview him ASAP while we've got him there! If he gets the all-clear, his mom won't have to be lonesome tonight, and I can drop him home in plenty of time to open Santa's stocking."

"Uh. Okay," muttered Todd, seeing that Lay-Zee boy disappear off into the far distance, fading away along with that cold slug of Bud in his mouth. It could be a long night. Sounded like Stan had the bit between his teeth again, and the race was on. Holidays or no holidays. He trudged back through the thickening snow towards the huge gothic structure he had wanted to avoid, and *had* escaped from.

Based on what Stan had heard from Amanda and Johnny, the evidence they already had, Bobby's past, and Stan's own instincts, Stan wanted this sorted out here and now – so drove them all to meet up with Todd at Weston State Lunatic Asylum.

In the back of the car, Johnny squeezed Amanda's hand. Goodness knows how she felt about going back to the asylum again – returning to the place of her callous treatment, but there had been no time for them to talk privately. Stan was oblivious to anyone's feelings and Johnny began to understand why Mandy wouldn't want a relationship with this man. He was single-mindedly intent on cracking this case. To hell with his girlfriend's feelings.

They passed the crumpled snow-covered shape of Todd's car against a tree off the road, barely visible through the snow storm, and Stan cursed. The snow was driving hard and had settled thickly underfoot by the time they reached the gates to the hospital. Stan's cruiser struggled up the driveway, crunching through the snow, which by then was halfway up the wheel trim.

"Dear Lord! Keep us safe!" William prayed aloud.

Eventually, they abandoned the car outside the hospital's main door, and Stan rushed inside. Johnny put his arm round Amanda, who had pulled her hood down low over her face. Whether it was to protect her from the heavy snow, hide her trauma, or ensure she wasn't recognized, Johnny didn't know, but it brought out the protector in him. They walked slowly up the steps, behind William's leggy figure.

Fortunately, Todd had managed to sweet-talk Mary-Lou into bringing down a doctor he could speak to. To this young female psychiatrist he had 'played the cop card' and got an immediate evaluation for Bobby at the asylum. She agreed to conduct the initial interview with Bobby, but Dr. Henry Cane would need to see him too for his evaluation later.

After that, Todd knew that Stan also wanted to interview Bobby Luellan just in case there was some truth to his witnesses' story, but there had been no need to tell the hospital staff that. It was police business.

"Yes, it's all arranged!" he shouted, as Stan burst through the front door into the reception area, looking around wildly, "Though why it's all so urgent, I don't know! We've got him."

"It's Christmas Eve. If he's harmless, I don't want to keep the poor dude locked up in the loony bin on Christmas Eve, for Chrissake!"

"Sheriff, please!" cried Mary-Lou admonishingly, and jerked her head to point out some patients who were shuffling past from one corridor to the next.

"Christmas Eve – for Christ's sake. Yeah. I hear ya!" sniggered Todd.

***

Outside the small bedroom, Henry Cane observed Bobby Luellan on the bed from a distance, as he stood staring through the glass panel in the door at the boy. It wasn't wise to get too close to out-patients currently under police custody. Since the young female doctor had done the basic paperwork and left to write up her conclusions, Cane preferred to invoke nightmares on the boy as he lay alone on the bed.

Of course, it wasn't even necessary for Cane to be within the proximity of Bobby, but the whole idea of experimenting on patients here in the hospital was that he could observe their bodily physical responses, as well as their psychological reactions. He loved to see absolute terror made manifest. And so he induced a sleep state on Bobby, and only stepped into the room when he was sure that Bobby was unconscious.

Bobby, meanwhile, was back in the nightmare room full of faceless Nazi soldiers; all faceless except for the one man that he recognized from somewhere, in pebble glasses, in the SS uniform, cruelly staring at him impassively. Bobby himself was lying spread-eagled on the bed, and realized that he was naked and unable to move. He started to panic, but it was as if everything was paralyzed, apart from his eyeballs which darted back and forth anxiously.

"Velcome to der End Times," the man said, in a German accent. But his lips did not move, and the voice appeared to be in Bobby's own head.

"Ve must eradicate das imbecile, und all of der intellectually incapacitated, lunatics, homosexuals, handicapped... End Times are here!" the voice boomed in his head.

The faceless Nazi soldiers all moved forward, each with a sharp dagger-like bayonet attached to the business end of their rifles. As they got closer, Bobby saw that their faces morphed into ghoulish decomposing flesh, the skin green and grey, eyes either bulging out grotesquely or missing, leaving black bloody holes that oozed pus. Bobby whimpered, but found himself unable to scream.

"One!" the men held their bayonets at the ready, their feet set apart ready to lunge.

"Two!" the men swung back their arms to give momentum to the weapons they held.

"Three!" the men thrust the bayonets into Bobby's flesh. He heard the sound first, and sort of 'chuck...' sound as the blades hit their mark, and in his initial split second of shock, he felt nothing, although he was aware that they had concentrated on his genital area. He heard the 'chuck- chuck- chuck- chuck' and wrench around and in his balls, his dick, and his asshole as the blades entered, and then more than excruciating pain as each man twisted their bayonet, shredding the flesh inside his most intimate areas, until his groin was a tattered red mess. Bobby screamed and screamed.

He had a vision of a river of blood, with decomposing corpses being washed onto the shore, piling one on top of the other, grey limbs entangled.

"End times..." said the calm, Germanic voice, as the SS officer with the inscrutable expression and distant eyes behind thick lenses, gently slipped a cold knife blade into Bobby's right ear, then began to bore and wriggle it into his skull.

Bobby screamed a long loud scream, but all the time it was drowned by a chant of "End times! End times! End times! End times!"

Bobby woke up in the small hospital room in a sweat, tears running down his face, just as the white coat of Dr. Cane swung out of the door. He held his face in his hands and cried.

Five minutes later, a nurse, instructed by the young psychiatrist, came to fetch Bobby. The female doctor had evaluated Bobby as a slightly odd, eccentric character, but since his IQ was quite low, this was to be expected. As far as she could see from initial analysis, he was not a danger to himself nor to other people, and despite Bobby having a tendency to enjoy raw food (and the doctor was fond of sushi herself), despite cultural taboos, and having had a nightmare last evening, the young psychiatrist could see nothing seriously wrong with him. And since Dr. Cane had just concurred with her evaluation, it was just a formality before he was released back into police hands. So, she told the nurse to fetch him down to the day room, and let him have a smoke or a breath of fresh air while she and Dr. Cane gave the police their findings.

The nurse found Bobby a little upset, but that was only to be expected. Lots of new patients were upset when they came here, but at least he was getting out fast, by the sound of it. She led him gently downstairs and into the day room, which had French doors leading into a covered courtyard. Further beyond that, was an open-lawn area surrounded by a chain-link fence, showcasing a beautiful view of the riverbanks beyond. They let some patients out here regardless of the weather, to have a smoke, or fresh air, and the teenager looked like he could use either. Bobby Luellan was outside, but still within the hospital compound, and could even wander a ways if he liked, since the area was contained. Quite safe and secure.

***

Back inside the hospital, Mary-Lou had shown the police and other visitors all into the staff room to wait, and rustled them up some coffees. Amanda sat with her hair swept over her face, peering between strands, afraid she might encounter Dr. Cane, her nemesis. As people came and went, with no sign of him, she relaxed a little. Evening finally settled in, with lots of snow still falling.

Staff who had just finished their day shift, and had tried to move their cars out of the parking lot to go home, came back into reception and on into the staff room, frozen, snowy, wet and exasperated. Their cars were covered in iced-over snow, under snowdrifts, and shovels had no effect. Their complaints drew the two policemen's attention, as well as that of Johnny, Amanda, and William.

"That's it then. Looks like freakin' Christmas in the asylum!" said one male healthcare worker, reaching for the staff telephone. "Oh, my wife will probably divorce me!"

"Christ!" exclaimed Todd, jumping to peer closer out of the window, "Don't say we are snowed in here!"

One of the nurses shrugged, "It's happened before! Though not on Christmas Eve. Mary-Lou's just rung the Department of Highways, but the two county snow ploughs are tied up on the main highways. There's no way they'll get here for hours – if at all. Damn these countryside asylums. We're not exactly emergency services or on a main road. Might have to settle in for the night!"

"What?" Stan roared, and stormed off to the reception desk to demand the impossible. Johnny and William shared furtive looks.

Amanda just shrugged in resignation. "It's not like I'd be sleeping in a strange place," she sighed, and Johnny put his hand on hers.

***

That evening, Bobby wandered off the courtyard, beyond the small huddle of smokers, and down into the snow, where it was pure and white. Of simple character, his mind skittered from thought to thought, and he had soon forgotten the trauma he had suffered from his recent nightmare. The snow delighted him. He grinned momentarily, remembering snowmen he had built, and an igloo once. He jumped in the snow with both feet, sinking into it to his knees, not caring that his jeans were soon soaked, and his legs began to sting with the cold.

The snow had momentarily stopped and it was a clear-white world; eye-achingly bright even though dusk was approaching. Bobby smiled as he surveyed the land, and spotted some tracks. *An animal*, he thought. Looked like a deer had been here, maybe. He began to follow, wading through the crisp, otherwise untouched snow. Parallel to the tracks, was a security fence, about ten feet high.

***

"Goddamn!" cried Stan, striding back into the staffroom, where the others were sharing cookies with the stranded staff members and were onto their fourth cups of coffee. "Turns out they've evaluated Bobby as dim but not dangerous and sent him out in the garden for a breath of fresh air, while I've been sitting here like a bozo! Come on Todd!" he grabbed his coat and swept out of the room, Todd scrambling up after him.

"More cookies for us," shrugged William.

***

Wonder if it's an electric fence? Bobby waded over to it, his hand reaching towards the fence, hoping he might sense the strength of it, wondering if it would kill him, or just give a mild shock.

He saw a piece of a 2x4 board lying near the fence. It appeared to have been part of a strut holding up a fence post that had broken off with the force of a snow drift. He wrenched it up and began to prod tentatively at the fence. He half expected to see waves of energy coming off it like in a comic book. He felt nothing. If it wasn't to keep people in, maybe it was to keep out…

He looked beyond the fence, and within a few feet, saw the banks of the river. Then – he screamed. And didn't stop screaming, and crying, "End times! End times!"

Because, reminiscent of his nightmare, through the chain-link fence he saw grey, ragged bodies being swept up and washed onto the riverbank a few feet yards away, limbs tangled, but worse, he saw them untangling themselves from one another on the land, and rising, scrawny limbs dripping and hair like weeds, cascading with brown river water, their horrific ashen faces turning their grey or blind eyes towards Bobby!

By the time the nursing staff had been alerted to Bobby's screams and ran towards the sound, Stan and Todd had joined them. They bounded across the snow with great difficulty, especially since a flurry of heavy snow had recommenced.

They attempted to run, sometimes plunging thigh deep in snow, which slowed their progress. Bobby continued, screaming, shouting, gabbling. They found Bobby catatonic in shock, banging repeatedly on the security fence with a hunk of wood, screaming, over and over again, and shouting, "End times! End times!"

"Christ! He's *not* dangerous, they say? He's *fine*? What the fuck!" exclaimed Todd, as the nurses held Bobby's arms and gently gave him a sedative shot.

"What the hell just happened here?" Stan asked. He stared through the fence in the direction that Bobby had been glaring wildly, but saw nothing through the large flakes of persistent snowfall but the white riverbank and the grey rushing river.

The staff half led, half dragged Bobby back to the hospital building, where his screaming had diminished to a wild gabbling about dead bodies and the frequently repeated, "End times."

"He's fuckin' lost it, Stan," Todd said, as they entered the hospital, the wall of warmth hitting them, "You won't get any sense out of him tonight!"

The smokers and other patients had been ushered in, the patio doors to the outside were locked against the night and patients were encouraged back to their rooms or the TV lounge. Such isolated occurrences and outbursts often distressed other patients, and the staff was trained to act to defuse the situation and regain the composure of the whole hospital.

The nurses led Bobby off to be examined by the night doctor – Henry Cane, they said – but it wouldn't be till after the doctor had made his planned rounds of the patients already on the wards.

"In the meantime, he can sleep it off in one of the rooms," a nurse reassured Stan.

"Terrific," he said, through gritted teeth.

William, Johnny, and Amanda looked up as Todd and Stan entered the staffroom, grim-faced.

"Well?"

"Kid's a raging lunatic," grimaced Stan, "At the moment, anyway. They've sedated him. He'll be unconscious shortly and later they're reassessing him. Fucking snowstorm's coming in worse. We could be here till shittin' New Year at this rate."

"Merry fuckin' Christmas, one and all," Todd flung himself into the plastic covered armchair, nearly knocking the coffee out of Amanda's hands.

"Language, please," said William quietly. "It's a holy night."

Todd glared at the boy in disbelief. Stan stared at him, also incredulous.

Amanda broke the silence, "Cookie?"

"Fucking insane, more like," grumbled Jonathan.

They fell into not very companionable silence, as the snow continued to fall outside.

The snowfall was as relentless as the group of grey-tattered figures outside the security fence, loosening the panel of fencing near the riverbank where Bobby had stood just minutes earlier. Their hands worked together, peeling up the strip of chain link where the rotten fencepost prop had been removed.

Bony, gnarled fingers stuck through the loops of the chains, clawed and crippled, some of them devoid of flesh, just milky bare finger bones working and worrying at the fence, catching the reflection of the moonlight on the snow. Almost beautiful, like twinkling Christmas lights.

CHAPTER 17

Ralphie made his way across the snow-deep field with grim intent, walking as best he could in the deep drifts, mindlessly driven by the forceful power of Legion within him, despite the lashing snow. The demon cursed the small body he was in at that moment and the circumstances that had brought him here. This was no appropriate vessel for supreme evil, thought Legion, blaming the Cane brothers' gross incompetence for his misfortune in having to stride crotch-deep through icy snowdrifts dressed in the body of a small boy. If demons could be thought to grumble, then Legion was doing so now, seething fit to melt the ice.

Unbeknownst to the demon – or to the essence of Ralphie that still remained – just an hour earlier a large semi-truck had skidded on the ice and ploughed into a utility pole, bringing down live power lines across the field; lines which were now buried by the persistent snow.

The emergency services had responded fast, keen to avoid further catastrophes on main highways in this weather, and the semi-truck had been towed. The driver had been taken to the hospital over in Clarksburg.

The power lines would take longer to fix, and some 'danger' tape strung across the outside of the fence was all the police could manage to do until the power company could take action. While the power was still running, and people weren't complaining, it wasn't a major priority for them – especially since many of the roads were still impassable. They would fix it as soon as they could. Meanwhile, the power cables lay in the snow, quietly buzzing with their thousands of volts, having seared their way through the snow drifts, now lying in ever increasing shallow pools of water.

Ralphie marched determinedly on, oblivious, eyes fixed to the distance. Wading awkwardly through the drifts, he was even grateful for the trench of more shallow snow he noticed ahead of him. He stepped fully onto the downed power line and was thrown twenty feet across the field and into the road.

He laid there, apparently unconscious. However, like a rechargeable battery, he was simply trying to figure out what happened; absorbing the 30,000 volts 'hit' he'd taken, which would merely re-energise him and only further increase his supernatural powers.

He lay, drinking in the strength, his body vibrating with the thrill of the energy surge, and basking in glorious comfort. He didn't even want to move to waste any of this good stuff until he felt completely revitalised.

By good fortune or bad, an ambulance happened upon Ralphie lying face down in the slush beside the road, only seconds after he'd been thrown over the fence by the force of the electric shock.

The ambulance was heading back to its base across town after a hospital trip to deposit the dazed and whiplashed semi-truck driver who had inadvertently caused Ralphie's present predicament.

"Stop!" cried one of the EMTs to his colleague who was driving. "We got another in nearly the same spot!"

A total of three EMTs rushed out, bent over the inert body to ascertain the risks of moving the 'unconscious' Ralphie, and stretchered him off into the back of the ambulance.

"He's cold," said one. "We need to check for hypothermia. Can't have been there long – we were just here!"

A pug-faced EMT then climbed in the back with Ralphie and set about checking his levels. While Ralphie was allegedly 'unconscious,' the force of Legion within his dead body imitated the heartbeat and vital signs of a live human sufficiently enough to deceive the EMT, who was satisfied that nothing was too greatly amiss with the small innocent boy who lay pale and unconscious beside him.

"OK! I got it, guys!" he shouted through the speaker panel to the cab and administered an oxygen mask to Ralphie, while the driver and the third EMT buckled into the front and headed to the hospital.

Meanwhile Ralphie overheard the EMTs talking amongst themselves in the front cab of the ambulance. They were heading towards the road which turned onto Weston State Lunatic Asylum, and passed a directional sign that set off a conversation. Ralphie listened to them intently.

"Lunatic Asylum!" said the driver scornfully, noticing the signpost. "Do people still call those hospitals 'lunatic asylums,' really? Can't believe that place still exists!"

One said, "Yeah, I was working the call when they brought Cathy Edwards in, once she'd physically recovered after her accident."

Ralphie's attention was sparked on full alert, although he pretended to be still unconscious, biding his time, and leisurely integrating the high levels of energy he had ingested.

"Accident? Didn't she step out into traffic? Suicide attempt?"

"Looked that way. She was so psychologically screwed up, they had to ship her off to Weston straight away. I was on that call to transfer her, unfortunately."

His colleague – the driver – interrupted. "That is one creepy hellhole, Man. Don't care what they say. If I was depressed or suicidal or whatever, that place would finish me off, for sure!"

"Uh-huh. Yup. Well that day was one of the weirdest I've experienced. Telling you... given that Cathy was a sweet woman, it was like she was possessed that day."

"Her family got killed – what d'you expect?"

Ralphie consciously forced himself to lie quite still, but the complex emotions he felt only confused him. He struggled to think what they were, these bubbling feelings in his stomach and chest. He identified that he was hurt and upset – thinking of his mom. He also felt terrific anger – although he couldn't explain why.

And, he was also hungry and tormented by the proximity of the pug-faced EMT. He kept bending over Ralphie's head to adjust the mask or dials attached to the tubes and electrodes monitoring his body. Ralphie's eyes subtly flicked open and watched the pulse throb in the man's neck, which tugged at something primal in Ralphie's unconsciousness. His nearness was filling Ralphie with a terrific yearning, the man's scent reminding him of the aroma and mouth-watering sensations of a roast dinner, like his Mom would make…

Ralphie struck. Suddenly, swiftly and silently, he sat up and bit hard into the throat of the EMT, who crumpled to his knees with a look of wide-eyed surprise and a strange, muffled gurgling sound. Having torn into the carotid artery, and feeling the warm gush of living blood on his tongue, Ralphie sucked and sucked in delight. He couldn't stop. He couldn't get enough. He was so thirsty. So hungry.

The driver was concentrating on carefully manoeuvring through the thickening snow, driving slowly for safety since he'd been reassured that the kid seemed stable, "She still in Weston after all this time - Cathy? Tell ya – that place would drive me insane, never mind cure me. One way ticket to hell, ya ask me…"

"Yep. Scary place, you're right. The night I went, I was nearly sorry to drop her off there at that sinister place. But Cathy was totally loony-tunes: gabbling, looking wild, in a strait-jacket – the works…"

"Hannibal Lecter job?" laughed the driver.

"You wouldn't be laughing, Eric – I tell ya. That big-old-spooky-mansion-house there, like Dracula's castle or something… gives me the creeps – and the staff are weird too."

"What? Mary-Lou?" the driver laughed. Mary-Lou was probably the friendliest person in town, and the first point of contact for the ambulance service, EMTs, and any visitors at all. She was born and raised in Melas, and everyone local knew her. She was as normal as it gets. "Mary-Lou? Yeah – she's weird shit!" the driver snorted.

"I'm taking about Cane, I guess. Doctor Cane's weird, for sure," the other EMT went on. "He's just plain strange. No empathy. They say that about psychopaths, don't they? It's like he should be one of the patients, locked up."

"Henry Cane? Pillar of the community – patron of charities – overall respectable dude?"

"Yeah, he gives that impression in public. But have you seen him in his own hospital? The cold look he gave poor Cathy chilled my bones. And the staff under him… they're all the same way – it's like they're under a spell."

"You make him sound like a Witch Doctor! He's been there years – and his record is spotless. Man. Now you're talking crazy!" he changed the gears down, trying to follow in the tire treads of other vehicles, but sliding slightly on the compacted snow.

"Something about his eyes... cold, I don't like."

"Something about your farts... stink, I don't like!"

The EMT who wasn't driving elbowed his colleague sharply in the arm. Then, as was his habit when he was the front passenger with a colleague and a patient in the back, yelled, "OK, Buddy?" over his shoulder. No answer. "Hey, Bud! You OK?"

Hearing no response, he then turned to the driver, asking, "What's the matter with him?"

The driver shrugged. The EMT shuffled round sideways to peer through the glass panel and cupped his hand to cut out the reflection. He reeled back in horror with a cry.

"What now?" scowled the driver, having swerved the steering wheel in shock at his colleague's outburst.

"Stop! Looks like Buddy's fainted, and the kid's started bleeding from the mouth! Quick, we better get in there!"

The ambulance crunched to a halt, and both men ran round either side of the vehicle and swung the rear doors open.

"Holy shit!" said the driver, who had almost disbelieved his friend's account of things. In fact, the reality was far worse than he could have imagined.

Their colleague had collapsed onto his side on the floor, deathly pale, and the little boy lay still on the gurney, an explosion of dark blood frothing around his mouth, as if he was haemorrhaging badly and had coughed up a pint. The situation appeared critical.

The men leapt inside the ambulance, slamming the doors behind them, offering shelter and privacy so they could attend to their patients, and sprang closer to bend over to get a better look at them, to take whatever action necessary to stabilize them both.

The boy looked closest to death, blood pouring from his open lips, and his abdomen was disproportionately swollen and bloated, they observed. He would be their first priority, as they both rushed to attend to him, leaning close, one prising open Ralphie's eyelid to peer at his pupil with a tiny torch, the other feeling the pulse in his wrist and checking the monitors.

Little did they know what to expect next, as Ralphie's now-open eyes focused coldly on the throat of the EMT leaning over him, quickly followed by his sharp teeth. At the same instant, his iron-strong little hand whipped round to the other man's wrist, thrusting his child's fingers straight through his skin and boring deep into the flesh beneath, holding onto the bones themselves in a vice-like grip. They hardly had time to scream.

Besides, the beautiful thing about snow is that it muffles everything.

When the snow falls softly in large flakes, especially on Christmas Eve, it gives people the urge to sit inside where it's warm, and eat and drink their fill; and for children to play in anticipation, while tingling with a thrill of excitement at what the day ahead holds. To Ralphie, in his own situation, and with his psychic knowledge and control of the ghouls' progress, that sounded like a Plan.

***

At Weston State Lunatic Asylum, now closed up for the night after the disturbance with Bobby, the patients too were preparing for Christmas. Some slept, or sat in their individual rooms, contented or unable to escape their own company. Others restlessly paced their small rooms or wandered the long dim corridors. Some paced or sat in the communal rooms for television, seasonal or non-seasonal activities. Those who didn't hold with Christmas and were active enough played pool or poker, or sat watching TV, or were knitting, sewing or reading.

The patients who were in a festive, friendly mood (or who were afraid to be alone) sat or danced in the huge tinselled recreation hall, under a twinkling faceted glitter ball, which revolved slowly, the lights trained on it making shafts of diamond light spark and explode onto the darkness beneath.

The room was dimly lit and sparsely furnished. Around the edges were paper-covered tables and chairs, leaving a cavernous space in the middle of the room for dancing or wandering aimlessly. Individual staff members grinned at depressed and blank faces, or chatted gleefully and inanely to people to inject some Christmas cheer.

Non-spiked fruit punch was the most potent drink available, since it was fairer not to discriminate against the patients taking drugs that were incompatible with alcohol, which was just about everyone.

Some of the care workers and nurses, dressed festively in paper hats, were leading an over-enthusiastic carol-singing session in one corner. Every so often, they took breaks from their singing to let an amplified CD player take over the role of disc jockeying Christmas songs, to which a handful of people shuffled in self-conscious approximations of dance. Mary-Lou's elderly father, Hank, would be arriving soon, dressed in his home-made Santa suit and a cotton-wool beard, to spread more joy to the desperately sad affair.

Although invited to join in the Christmas celebrations in the recreation hall, Stan, Todd, Jonathan, Amanda, and William politely declined the party invitation.

"Over my dead body," muttered Stan to himself between gritted teeth.

Most of the snow-stranded staff also declined. If they had to stay on the premises, they were unwilling to 'work' in their free time, especially late on Christmas Eve, which would have warranted double pay normally. No, if they were going to spend a miserable Christmas in the asylum, they were going to do it on their own terms. So the staff room was pretty crowded, and there was only coffee – decaffeinated or rocket-fuel – available to warm their hearts with Christmas cheer. That, and fruit punch, of course.

The very ill patients were being attended to in their rooms by the nursing staff and care assistants on duty. Dr. Henry Cane was on his rounds and all was right with the world.

Everyone was occupied, either in their own thoughts or what was going on in the building. Outside though, there was a different activity. The monstrous grey ghouls were occupied in getting into the building.

After they frightened Bobby into the hysterics that led to his enforced sedation, the ghouls had peeled up the chain link fence they had worried away from its holdings. Thanks to Ralphie's new-found psychic connection with these creatures and his ability to give them remote, rational instruction, they now operated with some intelligence. Moaning with fiendish excitement and success, the creatures scrambled beneath it, several of them catching their matted hair, scalps, rags and grey-papery skin on the sharp metal spikes of the torn thick wire edges, leaving grisly shreds of corpse flapping from the fence wire in the cold wind.

In the mines, the ghouls had been mindless and too stupid to even think of leaving the safety of the only home they knew, blindly wandering in the dark and containing themselves within a single mine shaft. Washed out into the outside world by the flood waters, they now had the scent of blood in their nostrils, and were under Ralphie's remote control.

With Legion's increasing power influencing them through the person of little Ralphie Edwards, the walking dead now had some intelligence controlling their actions. As a small but formidable army of the undead, they were a fearsome sight, and even more forbidding foes. But as yet, they lumbered unseen around the outside of the building, scratching at window frames, turning door handles, pushing fire exit doors. All were locked and impossible to penetrate from the outside, without a degree of cunning.

***

In his mind, as he drained and swallowed the last drops of blood from the last EMT, Ralphie was aware of the ghouls' attempts to gain entry to Weston. His psychically-connected intelligence bid them conceal themselves, to be more subtle than their brutish nature otherwise allowed. And therefore, he willed them to look to the basement entrances, the boiler room and heating vents and if need be, to kill their way into the building. Kill their way up, kill their way through, and kill their way out.

He laughed hysterically, throwing back his head, turning his freckled face up to the blood-spattered ceiling of the ambulance, and laughing through stained cherubic lips, wet to the chin with blood. But the sound that emitted from the little boy's mouth was not childish giggling. It was the thunderous deep roar of Legion's demonic voice, laughing psychotically, and so loudly that the metal ambulance walls shuddered with the deep vibration.

"But stay away from my Mom!" Ralphie willed the collective unconscious, with a firm glare.

***

"Crap!" Stan smashed the staffroom telephone into its cradle. "No telephone line now!" This day was going from bad to worse.

"Try your cell again!" snapped Amanda, irritated beyond belief. Stan's ill-temper was contagious and he was really getting on her tits (and not in a good way).

"I've still got no signal here," shrugged Jonathan, staring again at the iPhone in his hands.

William shook his head, unable to believe how so many people could be on the edge like this. He was bored, yes, like any teenager would be in these circumstances, but he didn't need to take a chill pill like these guys. Although if he decided that he wanted a chill pill, he figured he was in the right place, he smiled to himself.

"This is fuckin' ridiculous," muttered Stan, redialling the station again without even checking his signal strength, then putting the phone hopefully to his ear, "Still no fuckin' signal!"

"Bad weather," explained a male nurse, sucking his gums and staring into space.

"Don't say!" yelled the Sheriff, his temper worsening by the second. "Well, looks like I'm just gonna have to go out to the cruiser and use the radio." Stan made to push himself out of the low armchair.

"Wait, now, Stan. What for?" asked Amanda, "You've called in for snow plows every fifteen minutes since we got here and they said they'd be here ASAP. It's not like we're an emergency. What more can you do?"

"Kick their butts. Dig us out. Walk to the main road. Walk back to town," seethed Stan, frustrated.

"You want to go out in this?" said Todd, flicking his head towards the window and the heavy icy sleet which had now replaced the soft flakes. "Aren't we just comfy here, waiting?"

"No, I don't WANT to go out in it, officer," sneered Stan, sarcastically. "In fact, since you're so 'comfy' – you go! And that's an order!"

The audience in the staff room, who had fallen into silence as soon as the Sheriff raised his voice, now sat spellbound, gasping at the display before them.

"Where?" Todd choked on his eighth cup of coffee, wondering which of the range of suggestions he meant him to do – Stan surely couldn't mean him to walk all the way to the edge of town for help, and flag down a passing snow plow?

"You choose," said Stan. "I'm getting past caring. I just want some action here!" He ran his fingers through his hair, his face red.

"Stan, if you don't lay off, you're going to have a heart attack, babe," Amanda cautioned.

Johnny tried not to wince at the endearment she used on this boorish lout, and squeezed her hand. William noticed the gesture and its meaning and cast a calming look at Johnny. The last thing they needed now was some stag fight as if it were the rutting season.

Todd too had seen enough of dead deer for the night and stood up with determination. "OK, so I'll radio in for help. See if we can't get something happening," he sighed, and left the room.

Stan stood up and paced the room as far as he could, and back: "And when are they going to tell me the fuckin' kid's come round enough to interview, for fuck's sake? What a fuckin' waste of my time this has all been!" He kicked the leg of the chair he'd been sitting in.

Everyone sat in uncomfortable silence, the air heavy with tension.

"So... Sheriff," said one of the junior psychologists, taking his life in his hands, "How long have you had these anger issues?"

***

Ralphie stood up, hunched over the ambulance steering wheel, both feet firmly on the accelerator. It was the only way he could reach the pedal with these short legs, and see over the dashboard at the same time. Even for a nine year old, Ralphie Edwards had been small: a cute little poppet, but it made him a useless ambulance driver. The Legion within him cursed his plight again. Just wait till he saw Henry Cane!

The ambulance skidded and skied more than it actually drove through the tire tracks of previous vehicles. When Ralphie turned on to the Weston road the snow was far too thick to drive through because no vehicles had ventured down there for some hours now.

The ambulance got stuck, its wheels spinning helplessly as the engine roared. Ralphie jumped up and down on the accelerator in frustration, banging his head on the windshield in the process. Just as well he couldn't feel it.

"Fuck!" roared Ralphie in his Legion voice, along with the foulest stream of Satanic swearwords that ever set fire to a person's ears. He would have to abandon the ambulance here, after all. That meant he would have to plunge back into the snow and get wet, even if he sped Ralphie to Weston as fast as his stupid little legs would carry him.

Within Ralphie's tiny frame, Legion stepped out of the ambulance and into the snow again, resenting that Henry and Talman Cane had not had the intelligence to bring him fully into a physical being appropriate to his position. As Ralphie's small body began to trudge through the snow, Legion's mind bored into the brothers' brains with another torrent of demonic abuse.

This was no night for a nine-year-old to be out on his own.

***

Within the basement of Weston State Lunatic Asylum, all was not well. An external door swung gently off its hinges, flapping with an eerie creak, and letting in the flurries of snow, which had resumed again. The reflection of the outdoor security lights on the snow cast a dim glare into the basement area. On the floor, wet puddles and footprints, more like the

208

scrapes and drag marks of limbs, were to be seen on the linoleum. The basement was semi-dark, illuminated only by the dimly lit emergency night-lights, which buzzed from time to time as the ghouls dragged, limped, hobbled and jerked past.

They followed the big heating pipes across the room, deeper into the building, making a very sorry tattered procession towards a stairway and an internal door. Their bodies were now the worse for wear, after having been tumbled against rocks by the force of the river water that had landed them here, then dragging themselves through unwilling fences and doors, and their vain attempts to gain entrance to the building before they'd made it at last. Many had lost decayed fingers trying to prise open windows and doors, to no avail, until Ralphie had come to their rescue and introduced them to collective thought, so that they worked as one unit to one purpose: to kill.

***

Taking the least hazardous of the outdoor options open to him, Todd had trudged out the few yards to the cruiser, kicked away the pile of snow blocking the door, and was now standing outside, speaking on the police radio.

"I know. What can I say, Jocelyn? He's going stir-crazy here!" Todd idly palmed snow off the windscreen with his leather-gloved hand. "Yeah. Well, if you can get an actual time on that, maybe that'll… What the fuck?"

His bored glance into the mid-distance through the falling snow caught a dark figure crouching and disappearing beneath the building. Todd widened his eyes, unable to believe what he'd seen.

"Gotta go, Joss. Do what you can." Todd put down the radio and fixed his determined stare on the space where the figure had been, and began firmly wading through the snow in the direction he saw it disappear.

***

Weston State Lunatic Asylum was an old historic building, one of the first psychiatric hospitals of its kind in America, let alone in West Virginia. As such, its state-of-the-art building design was ground-breaking in the 1800s, but was deemed archaic and ineffectual now. The property was registered in the National Register of Historic Places, and the Trustees felt an obligation to preserve its original historical state as intact as possible, while serving the needs of its patients and staff.

The Board of Directors and staff had done what they could to modernize the place, with the least amount of structural disturbance and finance spent. Consequently, all walls were painted in cheap commercial paint bulk-bought in a restricted number of colours under the general overlying theme of 'faded.' The very long straight corridor floors, originally stone tiled, were now covered in a dull grey rubberised floor treatment, suitable for easy mopping rather than being easy on the eye. They had shut off one of the wings almost entirely, and had to leave it to decay, because the hospital's income only allowed them to maintain the working half of the building.

However, there was one room still occupied within the abandoned wing. The room nearest the double doors giving access to the main open wing was still in use, and housed Cathy Edwards. Dr. Cane had insisted that she remain in relative isolation there, although it would have made better financial and architectural sense to have cut off the wing right at the end where it joined the main open wing, at the double doors. The contractors had argued this, and the Board had earlier discussed the option. To retain the integrity of the building and provide the best insulation, it would make more sense to brick up the wing in its entirety.

However, Dr. Cane had recommended that an alternative arrangement was essential to the welfare of a vulnerable patient, and his research findings on this case study were generating great interest from prestigious medical publications. Dr. Cane was a force to be reckoned with – a popular, successful and renowned psychiatrist whose research work and reputation brought in a good deal of sponsorship, donations, grant funding, support, and paying patients – he generally got his own way.

A fibreboard partition in the corridor next to Cathy's room blocked off the deserted and unheated wing, but its freezing air permeated her walls, and the wind from broken windows howled through the wooden frame of the partition.

From one end to the other of the main hospital wing, the long hallways stretched out like a scene from a nightmare, with a regularity of identical doors on either side: all blank characterless mirror-images of one another, growing decreasingly smaller into the distance, like a lesson in perspective. Such an optical illusion and such a characterless environment were conducive to confusion and endless wandering and pacing. The only sounds generally emanating from the hallways and rooms were the low hum of the overhead fluorescent lights, and the moans and screams of the more insane that were locked in their rooms for their own safety and for that of others.

Most of the patients' residential rooms were contained within this single wing, apart from Cathy's room in the adjoining abandoned wing. There was a very distant sound of Christmas music from the recreation hall through the double doors and across the entrance area.

Still, the hospital was a stark and grim old place, and you didn't need to have missed your dose of hard-core anti-psychotic drugs to believe that you saw things lurking in dark corners taking up residence in the facility. You didn't need to be mad here, but it helped.

Rumor had it that the place was haunted by the miserable souls of former patients and the strange doctors who had experimented on them here. They had performed crude brain surgery, lobotomies and trepanning – making holes in people's skulls to let out 'bad vapours' and release pressure. Dr. Cane still

212

advocated tying patients to beds, electric shock therapy and worse. People said that you could hear the ghostly sound of the deceased souls in torment if you listened very carefully in the dead of night. Even some of the staff had occasionally been freaked out by shadows in the dark.

But tonight, on this silent night, holy night – all was calm, all was bright.

***

One patient sat on the narrow bed in his room, gazing lethargically at the wall, until his door burst open and a ragged, grey-skinned female figure flew at him, throwing him back on the bed. What was left of her face was grotesquely disfigured, with one desiccated eyeball dangling from the black hollow of her eye-hole.

He whimpered in fright, uncertain of his thinking and position on the fine line between his reality and his own psychosis. But after initial frozen shock, his excruciating pain was real enough. She ripped out his throat in one deft movement, causing a fountain of blood to spray over the ceiling and wall, and began to suck furiously at his throat before the pumping of his blood was lost as he died. The appalling slurping sound and the coppery stench of blood brought in another of the grey creatures, and they both feasted upon the poor man's body; the second ghoul horrifically licking the splashes of blood off the wall and floor where it had pooled, with a long greenish-grey tongue the color of fungus, now tinged with scarlet blood.

***

Cathy stared out her window and watched the snow fall down. Soon, the doctor would be in, as usual, to go over her meds and to see if things were a little bit better this evening.

Of course, nothing was ever going to be completely better – and being committed to an insane asylum certainly didn't make matters any better for her. At least things were getting a little more comfortable. For an entire two months, she had not needed a straitjacket to restrain her. She was even allowed to eat meals with her own hands, and using real blunt knives and forks, in actual metal, like a proper human being. For a while the staff feared her injuring herself with the silverware.

This afternoon was very nice. A choir from the Weston Presbyterian Church had been in and sang Christmas carols to the patients. They even brought cookies for the patients. Cathy's cookies were still on her nightstand, untouched.

Looking back at the snow building up on the window-sill, Cathy thought that it looked like it would be a white Christmas after all. Bing Crosby would be happy.

A gentle tap on the door; Dr. Cane must be here. He was always nice to her, and she felt safe with him. Dr. Cane was an older man in his sixties who wore wire-rimmed glasses and reminded her of John Lennon. She sometimes asked him when his band was getting back together and he would kindly remind her that the Beatles would not be getting together anytime soon. This was especially true since Mr. Lennon had been killed, but when Dr. Cane reminded her of that fact, she usually told him that was hogwash.

Dr. Cane came in with a smile on his face. "I have a visitor for you this evening, Cathy."

"Oh, that's nice; but send them away. I'm not buying anything," Cathy said sarcastically.

"The young man has a present for you," Dr. Cane replied pleasantly. "It is Christmas and all." Then in a whispered voice he added, "He's just a little boy. It is very brave of him to visit a place like this in the evening. Most young folks simply have too many things to do. It's Christmas Eve; most kids are with their families. Please be grateful and receive this young man."

"Sure, whatever," Cathy replied, uninterested. "Send him in."

Cathy picked up the plate of cookies and contemplated eating one or offering one to the visitor.

A young boy cautiously walked through the door. He was carrying a package wrapped in green foil with a red ribbon around it.

As soon as he stepped into the full light of the room, Cathy dropped the plate of cookies on the floor.

"Ralphie! Oh, my God!" she screamed. Her mind reeled. This couldn't be.

"Hello mom," he replied, eyes glowing wildly. "It's been a long time."

***

Todd shined his flashlight at the snow outside the broken basement door and noted the trampled footprints in the compressed snow. Either one person had been stamping around, keeping warm, or there was a whole crowd of intruders. *Or escaped lunatics.* He wondered.

He swung the flashlight's beam to the trench of flattened snow which snaked around the edge of the building, towards the perimeter fence, then swung it back and stepped inside the basement, noting the muddy pools, wet prints and scuffle marks on the floor. In horror, he spotted something and peered closer, shining the light on the mark he was scrutinizing.

A bare foot? He took another look. That was definitely a bare footprint, with a shaped sole, and toe prints. Only three toes, though. *Damn! If this was a homeless person, it was a wonder all their toes hadn't been frostbitten right off. Looked like they'd brought their friends with them, though. Where the hell from? They were out in the middle of nowhere here. It wasn't like they were in a city with an underpass.*

Then he thought about the abandoned wing of the hospital. That would be ideal for anyone wanting to take shelter in this godforsaken place. A funny place for a whole gang of homeless people to congregate, but it wasn't beyond the imagination. Chances were that old unheated wing had got so icy that they'd sought the heat of the boiler room and basement. Still, if there was more than one of them, Todd wasn't about to investigate without backup. He went out the way he came in, and made his way to the main entrance.

***

The ghouls had an uncanny nose for living human flesh, even though several of them had actually lost their nose structures, and wore only skeletal holes or ragged cartilage, devoid of skin and flesh. They cast their cataracted gazes or bloated black orbital pits from side to side, scanning the rooms, homing in on the locked or closed doors behind which vulnerable patients attempted to improve their mental health. The ghouls looked blind, but somehow, they saw, even in the dark outside, as they had done in the depths of the mines. The dim light of the hallway led them to their prey. That, combined with the homing instincts that Ralphie's psychic connection had given them and the primal senses they retained.

They followed the scent of life, and left death in their wake. From room to room, they gorged themselves, and rarely did anyone put up much of a fight. Most of the patients were sedated in some way; some were so terrified that their throats closed up and no sound was released: they screamed inwardly, with rasping in-breaths that alerted no one.

217

Those who managed ear-piercing screams fared no better. The staff were well used to moaning and screaming from many of the patients. When a member of staff occasionally patrolled the hallway, and checked on a room or came to the assistance of a particularly distressed patient, the ghouls silently ambushed them and committed them to the same fate as the patients.

The creatures of the night worked as a team, in pairs or alone, making their way down the corridors. Sometimes a group of them would fall upon the unsuspecting soul and tear him limb from limb, guzzling on the flesh and blood, and picking at their bones. They were insatiable. Some of them had not fed for years, and were making up for it now.

At other times, individual ghouls simply sucked out their victims' blood from the most convenient artery or vein, and left it at that, as if they were simply sampling the gravy of a roast dinner and pushing the plate aside to go onto the next course. There were many other victims to feast from, after all.

These mindless creatures did not have the sophisticated thinking processes to make that choice, of course; they were driven merely by a lust for blood, and flesh was simply dessert – if they wanted it. Ralphie's remote thinking and the power of Legion controlled them as a General might control an army. They moved as a unit, each one individually or collectively contributing to the overall drive to kill. The blood they consumed and the souls they freed into

218

Hell all fed Ralphie's and Legion's evil strength, increasing their power with every soul that was taken.

And in the residential main wing, as the ghouls worked their way steadily up the corridor, they left an increasing body count in their wake. The inert corpses of patients and staff lay in disarray inside the rooms: some on the floor, others slumped across beds and other furniture. It became like the fairy tale castle where the evil witch casts a spell and everyone falls asleep.

***

"Sleep in heavenly peace, Sleep in heavenly peace!" the words of the latest carol in the recreation hall sounded out clearly as Todd burst into the staffroom, but stayed in the doorway, holding open the door.

"Stan – I need a word, please. In private?" Todd beckoned with a jerk of his head for the Sheriff to follow him outside.

Stan, already on his feet and pacing the room, frowned, but followed him out of the door.

"Guy's a jerk, Mandy," muttered Johnny, glad of some time with Amanda without the tension of Stan being around. He looked around the staffroom again, spacious enough, but now filled with staff from day shifts who couldn't get home, who sat looking like sullen refugees, and odd duty staff on breaks, still brisk and business-like.

"He wasn't always like this, Johnny," Amanda said. "It's this case. But he's got even worse than last time I saw him. It's like it's driving him mad."

"You can say that again," Johnny folded his arms.

"It's driving him mad," repeated Willie, and winked as Johnny scowled at him.

***

"Silent night, holy night! Shepherds quake at the sight!"

"Homeless people, Todd?" Stan said doubtfully, following him across the reception area, " Didn't you just move them on? Or this weather, Christmas cheer and all, maybe the caretaker and hospital authorities would have offered them some shelter anyway?" He was beginning to think Todd was a pussy, asking for backup for this. "How many of them?"

"Never saw them. Just saw the marks."

"The marks? What the hell are they? Graffiti? Smears of feces on the walls? What?"

"Just footprints, quite a lot of them, in the basement."

Stan's first flicker of doubt began to flare. "Then you ought to question your assumptions, Todd. Who says we're dealing with homeless people anyway?"

"Who the hell would break into a lunatic asylum anyway? It ain't gonna be the patients, is it?" Todd grumbled.

They crunched through the compressed snow of the entrance and across the front of the building, reusing the footsteps that Todd had made just a few moments before, to enter the building.

Arriving at the basement door, Stan could see immediately that the door had been busted off its hinges.

"Unlawful entry," Stan muttered. He wished he had Todd's simple assumption that vagrants had caused this, but he had a sick feeling in his gut that the situation might not be as straightforward as that. His instinct told him there was something terribly wrong here.

They entered the basement, now layered with snow at the entrance, where the footprints were all but obliterated. Just a damp, muddied, occasionally puddled trail. To Stan, it looked like a body had been dragged through here. Or several.

His right hand on his service weapon, he shone his flashlight and Stan and Todd followed the trail through the dimly lit basement.

***

A curly-haired, uniformed nurse entered the staffroom, bringing with her the sound from the hall: "Glories stream from heaven afar!"

She scanned the staffroom. "Anyone seen Sandra?" she called. Those who heard her shook their heads.

She shouted across to another nurse on duty, who was just filling her coffee cup, "Shirelle! Did you see Sandra? She was just going to check the main rooms, then coming on her break. But that was nearly an hour ago. You seen her?"

Shirelle shook her head. "No, but maybe she went back via the main wing?"

"Sandra ain't been in at all, Carol," said the male nurse who should have been home by now. "I should know. Been sittin' here hours myself!"

"Strange," said the nurse, "but I've never known Sandra miss out on her caffeine kick before! Weird!" she shrugged. "Okay, so I'll try the main wing!"

She left the room.

William was counting the rosary, bent over with his head slightly bowed, kissing the beads. Amanda stretched over and tousled his hair. This time, he didn't mind the affectionate gesture: she was his aunt, after all.

"You OK, honey?" she asked. "It's not like it's Sunday, you know."

"God is for every day, not just for Sunday," William admonished, mildly.

Amanda raised her eyebows. "OK – you're just not the cheeky little boy I remember, Willie. I'm surprised, is all!"

William shrugged, tight-lipped and defensive.

Jonathan came to his rescue. "We all grow up. Willie has refound his faith. Maybe it's the strict Catholic school he goes to, maybe it's his way of mending his ways after being sent to the Home. Perhaps it's the experiences he's gone through. Believe me – they were intense, and I was there.

Whatever, we can use all the help we can get in the battle against evil."

Amanda looked at him seriously, with consideration. She felt as if she was the only one who didn't know what was going on here, but she had to trust Johnny and Willie on this. They had gone through so much. But the one thing she had going for her was that she knew Weston Lunatic Asylum inside out. And if she ever saw Dr. Henry Cane again... she wouldn't be responsible for her actions.

Jonathan was feeling more and more uneasy about this situation. In his own way, he was as restless as Stan. He didn't like this one bit. But unlike Stan, he had kept his emotions to himself, and focused his frustration on planning for the worst-case scenario.

***

Someone had opened a window in the recreation hall, and the sound permeated into Cathy Edward's room. The voices singing in the hall had swelled with those stranded staff who thought they might as well get in the Christmas spirit and join in the celebrations:

"Heavenly hosts sing Alleluia!

Christ, the Saviour is bo-orn! Chri-ist, the Saviour is born!"

Ralphie shuddered in disgust, "I hate that fucking song," the voice of Legion rumbled deeply out of Ralphie's mouth. It was in a whisper by Legion's standards, but shocking enough for Cathy.

"W…what did you say, Ralphie?" Cathy said, wide-eyed.

"I coughed, Mommy," said Ralphie sweetly, holding his throat, and giving a childish deep cough, simulating the same sounds as before: "Ahaa – tha – faaka – ss – ann-kk!"

Even the morbid blank face of Dr. Henry Cane gave the flicker of a smirk.

"Darling, I'm not surprised, if you've been out in that weather," she placed her hand on Ralphie's forehead. "You're icy cold as it is. You'll catch your death."

Ralphie rolled his eyes at Dr. Cane.

Cane sat down in Cathy's visitor chair, and settled himself as if he might be in for a long stay. He was keeping out of the way of both the ghouls in the main wing and the cops in the reception and activity wing. He was unafraid: it was just simpler not to complicate things, and to avoid unnecessary confrontation. It could all go on without him, after all. Ralphie was the key.

Faced with the sight of her little boy again, Cathy had all but forgotten he had died. It was all in the distant past, and so much had gone on since then, she wasn't sure what had been reality and what was delusion. All she cared about was that her son was with her again, and she accepted him, unquestioningly.

Cathy cuddled Ralphie close to her, and the little boy in him relished being back with his mother. But with every person killed by the ghouls in the next wing, Legion's strength grew within him. Although they were in control of the ghoul army, Ralphie still did not want his mother to be put in any danger, and Cane wished to avoid any encounter too. He had an uneasy feeling that Legion was not averse to punishing Cane in some way, despite their supernatural links and Cane's position as son of the Master. Best they all keep out of the way of the ghouls until this was over.

"We'll just stay nice and safe in here, won't we, Dr. Cane?" Ralphie smiled, swinging his legs, which dangled over the side of Cathy's bed. "Because we don't know what's going on outside, do we?"

Cane raised his eyebrows behind his wire-rimmed glasses, and folded his arms.

Ralphie continued, "But we all know it's for the best!"

***

"Silent night, holy night, Son of God, love's pure light!"

Stan and Todd, shining their flashlights into corners, had drawn their weapons as they pressed further on into the basement, creeping quietly through the pipe-lined depths, following the wet trail before them. Their flashlight caught a doorway, and they nodded to one another, and moved forwards.

The last thing they expected was a body to come flying down from the top of a heating pipe near the ceiling. It hit Todd with a dull thud, bringing him down immediately, cracking his skull on the concrete floor. Stan responded immediately with a shot to the arm, which did not deter the creature at all from savaging Todd, so he had no choice but to shoot for the head.

To his horror, this dark figure was still not even incapacitated by a shot to the head, and merely cast a vague sightless glance towards Stan, as if mildly irritated by a mosquito bite, rather than a lethal bullet through the brain.

Its face was grotesque: grey-ragged skin dropping off its face, and bones showing through the rips. A vicious row of jagged teeth showing as it gaped open mouthed. It was then that Stan truly realized what he was faced with: a gruesome zombie-like creature that could not be killed with bullets. In split-seconds, Stan's mind flashed with all the traditional horror-movie ways to stop creatures of the night: silver bullets? Beheading? Staked through the heart?

The quickest thing he could think to do was pistol-whip the creature, which merely sent it momentarily reeling off Todd's unconscious body. Then Stan spotted a metal spade leaning against the wall, presumably left from attempts to clear the snow. He grabbed it and swung at the creature, hitting it resoundingly in the face with the flat of the shovel-end. It fell on its back with the force of the strike, and Stan slammed the blade down onto the creature's neck, cutting a jagged trench into its throat, that gave out a thick, Jell-O-like blood, clotted and curdled with green. Still, the creature struggled to get up, its head hanging sideways, half-severed from its body, hanging by skin and sinew, greasy ropes of hair dangling down by its side.

Stan swallowed down the rising bile in his throat and swung again at the dangling head, this time striking it off completely. The body crumpled to the floor without a twitch.

Panting and trembling with fear and exertion, Stan bent over Todd and checked him over. He was breathing, and Stan touched his neck. There was a pulse, and as if to confirm he was still living, Todd's eyelids flickered open and eventually focused on Stan.

"You okay?" asked Stan.

"I've been better," said Todd, sitting up and holding the back of his head, wincing.

***

"Radiant beams from Thy holy face.

"With the dawn of redeeming grace…"

The curly-haired nurse, Carol, left the reception area behind her, and let herself through the double doors with her pass card and into the residential wing. The corridor was completely quiet, and no one was to be seen.

"Hello?" she tested, stepping towards the first room. It was Emmie Waters' room, a pleasant young woman of twenty-three, who was in for clinical depression, and doing well.

Carol knocked at the door and opened it, "Hi Emmie!"

Emmie looked up from her iPad, lounging on the bed as she often did in the evening, "Hi Carol!"

"You okay? Want to come over to the rec hall? Sing some carols? Drink fruit punch? Dance?"

Emmie looked at her, askance. "Seriously, Carol? I'm depressed! Do you actually want me to kill myself?"

Carol rolled her eyes and scolded her. "Emmie-you *were* depressed. Not now! Get into that positive frame of mind."

"OK. I positively don't want to spend Christmas with a load of sad losers."

Carol gave up. "Have you seen Nurse Harper, Emmie? You know – Sandra?"

"Nope," said Emmie, not even glancing up from her iPad.

"Thank you for your help." Carol closed the door behind her.

It was strange not to see anyone on the corridors. There were usually at least half a dozen members of staff walking the corridor, and more hanging around the nursing station half way down the hallway. Strange.

She walked down towards the nursing station. Then – there was a muffled blast in the distance, as if underground. And another! Was that gunshots? What the hell? Was that sound coming from the basement? Her mind hurtled around possibilities: the heating? Had a boiler exploded? But the noise she'd heard sounded like distinct cracks, like gunfire, not an explosion.

She quickened her pace towards the nursing station, in an alcoved room half way along the lengthy

228

corridor. There was still no one to be seen. She picked up the phone and rang through to Mary-Lou on reception. Fortunately, the internal phone system was still operational.

"Mary-Lou? Are those cops still there? Yeah?... When?" She listened, a sense of urgency growing within her.

Carol's heart began to race. "Well, when they get back in, you might want to send them this way!" She explained what she'd heard and asked for some of the staff to come back from their breaks.

"It's like the Marie Céleste here," she explained to Mary-Lou. "You know, that ship where they just found everything set for dinner, and nobody around... Or the Bermuda Triangle. Something's not right. OK. Yes, please. Just get them here. Do something, please."

She put the phone down and walked back up the corridor the way she'd come in. She had an uneasy sense that she wanted the staff to work in pairs. But here, she couldn't even see one member of staff.

Then Harlan Mill's room door opened, and a white-coated figure stood there. It was the medical doctor, Dr. Lockyer, who worked in tandem with Dr. Cane. Dr. Lockyer's specialism was pharmacological interventions. He was into drugs, whereas Dr. Cane's interest was physical and psychological therapies.

Carol just caught a glimpse of him as the door opened, but she was so relieved to see him that she exclaimed, "Oh, thank God!"

Dr Lock's body slid gently down the door to the floor, to her surprise, and it was then that Carol noticed that the left hand shoulder of his white coat was covered in blood, and his throat gaped open, glistening.

Carol screamed and screamed.

Until something stopped her, abruptly.

***

Johnny had stepped out of the staffroom telling Amanda and Willie he was just out for a change of scenery, but he really wanted to see if he could get an idea of what was going on. Stan and Todd had left in a hurry there, and they were nowhere to be seen. Johnny didn't have a good feeling about this.

When he saw the bunny-in-the-headlights look on Mary-Lou's face when she got that internal phone call, his unease increased. He popped his head back into the staffroom and called out for Amanda and William to join him in the reception area.

Mary-Lou wasn't the type to over-react, but she thought she had better take matters into her own hands. She hadn't liked the tone of Carol's voice on the phone: afraid and uncertain. Carol was a highly experienced senior nurse, and she had never heard her sound like that before. Plus – she mentioned gunshots! Her calling for the handful of staff on their break to return to the main wing wouldn't help if there was a crazed gunman in the place. And she didn't know where the two cops had gone.

Marty-Lou rushed to the front door, but couldn't see them anywhere. They hadn't headed for the cruiser, half submerged in snow – she could see that, although there were some other tracks outside. But she was wearing her polished court shoes, and didn't want to step too far out on the icy front door step. Her snow boots were back in her locker in the staffroom. There was no way she would be running around outside in the snow, looking for Stan and Todd.

Johnny went up to the desk, waiting for Mary-Lou to step back in. He saw the anxious look on her face, and the way she nibbled her lower lip, distracted.

"Have you seen Stan and Todd?" Mary-Lou said urgently. "Stupid... I mean, I know they went out. I saw them go. D'you know where they were going?"

"I was going to ask you the same thing!" said Johnny.

"Oh!" Mary-Lou squeaked, "I know they went out, but we really need them! There were shots, tell them! Coming from the basement."

Amanda put her hand on Johnny's arm, but he was oblivious. "Where does the basement give out onto the first floor?"

"Oh. Several places. The basement runs under the whole complex. The main wing..." Mary-Lou wasn't reassured by Johnny's determined look, and her anxiety was growing to hysteria.

At the same time, an ear-piercing scream emanated from the direction of the main wing, and persisted, again and again.

231

Mary-Lou's eyes widened in terror. No police in sight, she thought the best thing she could do was to set off the alarm.

As the klaxon sounded, people spilled into the reception area, from the staffroom and the recreation hall, looking bewildered. In the absence of anyone in a better position to take control, Jonathan knew he would have to step up to the plate.

"OK! Everyone!" he yelled above the bustling, querulous crowd, "Into the Rec Hall!"

Noisily muttering amongst themselves with each person engendering panic in another, the crowd of patients allowed themselves to be hustled in to the recreation hall, where the lights were switched on.

Jonathan held his hands in the air to call for silence, and although there were still some whimpering and sniveling sounds from the frightened patients, Johnny had sufficient silence to make an announcement.

"OK folks!" he said, as upbeat as he could. "We are going to have us a fine old Christmas party here, but it is essential that nobody leaves this area. The other wings are off-limits – OK? If staff could assemble, at the front here, we will brief you on your role. We will explain to everyone as soon as we can, but we are going to have to contain you here for some serious Christmas partying – all night if need be! Please bear with us, staff and patients, and I thank you for your co-operation! Maestro – hit the music!"

An upbeat Christmas song struck up through the amps, and the chattering crowds uneasily began to drift to the chairs and tables at the sides of the room, while some clusters stayed to dance in the middle.

"Oh, well – at least it looks like more of a party now," said one of the off-duty staff who had volunteered their time in the hall. The numbers had swelled by 300% with everyone from the other activity rooms and the staffroom, all in the hall now.

"Merry Christmas!" said old Hank, through his cotton wool beard.

***

When Stan and Todd burst up through the basement door into the corridor of the main wing, they saw in the distance a curly-haired nurse screaming hysterically. They ran to her and Stan grabbed Carol's shoulders. She stopped screaming, shocked by the blood-spattered Sheriff, carrying a gory spade, and the disheveled deputy, but relieved to see them.

Up the corridor, towards the main double doors, heads popped out of rooms and patients wandered into the corridor to see what was going on. Down the corridor, though, all was silent and doors remained closed. There was a distinct demarcation line between inhabited rooms from which patients emerged, unsettled and curious, and ones with blood-smeared doors, closed upon the atrocities inside.

Stan had noticed the bloody hand-print on one door, and looked inside. He nearly puked at what he saw lying spread-eagled on the floor. A half-eaten body: no flesh or skin left at the neck, chest or abdomen; rib-cage and spine exposed, and the remains a bloody mess; entrails lying pulled out like freshly made sausage, pale and expansive across the blood stained carpet. No one else to be seen.

But where were the creatures now? Somewhere between the rooms of the dead and the rooms of the living. They had been working their way systematically up the corridor, like a grim tide, and Stan was uncertain how far they had reached. They must be somewhere in this middle land of rooms, keeping quiet in the hubbub.

"Get those patients out of here!" yelled Stan across the patients in the corridor to Carol in the distance, and, although still in shock, she snapped to attention, and began bustling the patients towards the double doors which accessed onto the reception and activity areas.

Todd, still not quite recovered from his head injury, and rubbing the back of his neck, helped to shepherd people from their rooms, banging on doors as they went. "Hey! Come on out, there!"

Carol pushed ahead to present her pass card to the electronic reader, allowing people off the wing. The patients crowded through the double doors like a sea of bodies, and joined a terrified Mary-Lou in the reception area. She directed them to the Rec Hall.

It was only as the frightened crowd spread into the wider reception area, after funnelling through the double doors, that anyone realized that two of the grey skulking creatures had joined them, squeezing in shoulder to shoulder between the single-minded patients, focused only on escape.

With horror, Emmie Waters stepped back and saw that her bustling companion was a grey-skinned, tattered ghoul with cataracts on its unseeing eyes, razor sharp teeth and a stench of decomposing flesh. There were hysterical screams, and the two hideous creatures hissed and spat, standing back to back, judging their next move.

The patients stampeded every which way – some into the hall, some bursting outside into the snow. One patient fainted on the spot and two others stood frozen, too petrified to move.

Carol pushed them, but they were catatonic. The two ghouls fell upon them immediately, ripping out their throats, and spraying Carol with hot blood. She screamed and ran off to the staffroom, covered in blood.

Back at the main wing, in the no-man's land of rooms somewhere between life and death, Stan was kicking in doors, his hands held firmly on the bloody spade. He had already dispatched two more ghouls he found hiding in bedrooms, with some hefty kicks and chops to the neck, wielding the shovel blade as a weapon. He was exhausted, living off adrenaline, and had no idea how many more there were to tackle.

***

Johnny had briefed his small army of staff, taking those who wanted to know the facts into the staffroom.

He didn't know exactly what to expect himself, but he very much suspected some kind of vampire activity.

"Trust me on this, however hard it is for you to believe," he addressed the staff, explaining his suspicions and the methods they would use to stop whatever was working its way up from the basement. After hearing his words, several of the staff had chosen to fight, rather than await the inevitable. Some decided to take their chances out in the snow, and fled for their lives, promising to call for help as soon as they reached the roads, or got a signal on their cell phones. The others were aware of the situation, but chose to attend to the patients and ensure that no panic occurred. They went back to the hall, swallowed their fears, smiled at the patients and hoped for the best.

Johnny's army had managed to gather a small artillery together, too. They had a long-handled log chopping ax, two emergency fire axes, carving knives, shovels and a garden scythe. Someone had brought all the garlic they had from the kitchen, but Johnny shook his head doubtfully. The intense and powerful evil they were dealing with wouldn't be put off by a few cloves of garlic, whatever the vampire films said.

The rest of the staff turned their hearts and minds to pretending everything was fine. They were going to play the music real loud and distract the patients as much as possible from wondering what was going on. They would party as if their lives depended on it. Which, in a way, they did.

Hank the Santa, oblivious, was having a really good time, bobbing along on the dance floor, with women tugging at his beard, and men bouncing off his belly. The party was now actually much better than the sad affair it had been, since everyone who had avoided it was now here. Some, affected by the crowds, music and laughter, actually began to add to the atmosphere, and danced around. It was actually the best party that hall had ever seen, despite the underlying question in the heads of the patients – why couldn't they go anywhere else?

As Johnny's army, armed to the teeth, prepared for battle, the disco blared, and the crowds had emerged from behind the double doors of the main wing. Hysterical screaming and Carol's entrance brought Johnny's group out from the staffroom, to see two creatures savaging two patients.

The brave army momentarily looked on in horror. Somehow the reality of the situation was more daunting than they'd expected, but Johnny and William, used to dealing with the forces of evil, sprang into action. Johnny swung the long-handled ax and chopped into the neck of one creature. Willie ran up and hacked at another with a fire ax. They both needed extra chops, but soon, the creatures lay dead on the floor in a pool of the blood they'd drunk, surrounded by screaming and crying staff and patients.

The members of the armed team Johnny had employed gulped down their own terror at their leader's demonstration of what it took to defeat these beasts, and followed him and William with trepidation through the double doors into the main wing.

Carol's professionalism had taken over from her personal fear, and she bustled the handful of hysterical patients into the staffroom. She wanted to isolate this group from those evacuated patients who hadn't witnessed the scene and from the happy people in the Rec Hall, whose music was too loud for them to have heard. This would confine the panic to one small group. She would give them the necessary tranquilizers to calm them down, and decided she would pop a couple herself.

***

Having his forehead stroked by Cathy, Ralphie's body felt fine, but his mind, controlled by Legion, was in turmoil. This was not right! What the hell was happening out there? He was psychically aware that several ghouls had been discovered and killed, and he was not happy. Not a happy little boy at all.

There were enemies in their midst.

He scowled at Henry Cane, his eyes glowing red. Cane sat with his arms folded, and his lips firmly pressed together in dissatisfaction, staring coldly through his wire-rimmed frame. Legion's thought-form burst into Cane's brain, dragon-like, and his meaning was clear.

At this rate, this was not going to fulfill the Great Plan, and put into motion the End Times, as was foretold. They had sat here for long enough, leaving those half-wit creatures to do most of the groundwork, and now it was time for action.

Ralphie shrugged off his mother's hugs and shuffled himself off the bed, standing on the floor. It was time he went out there and made himself known.

***

Stan and Todd stood in the middle of the main wing's hallway, having killed two more ghouls. Stan panted, breathless and sweating. He had done most of the work wielding the weapon, and Todd had merely cornered the creatures in the rooms. Half-heartedly, in Stan's opinion, although Todd was probably still suffering from his earlier encounter and his head injury. God, Stan was exhausted. He had grabbed a jug of water from the last bedroom and swigged it back in one, before pressing on down the corridor, sweat streaming through his eyebrows and into his eyes.

"OK. This could be the last room. I remember people coming out of the ones further up, but we'll do a sweep anyway, OK?" Stan opened the door and found it empty. Just to be sure, he and Todd stepped inside to look around and under the bed, in the wardrobe – all the usual places they checked in every room.

Stan bent to flick his flashlight under the bed. "Clear!" he said, and stood up.

When he turned round, Todd was right in his face.

"What's up, buddy?" said Stan, puzzled. "We could be home free from here on!"

"Mmmm," murmured Todd, "I feel a bit…" He bit hard into Stan's neck, and held on, like a pit-bull. Stan tried to push him off, but succeeded only in ripping down the collar of Todd's shirt, where he saw two dried-blood fang-marks on the base of Todd's neck.

"Oh, God!" thought Stan, as he lost both blood and consciousness. "The ghoul in the basement bit him after all!"

***

Jonathan stepped carefully into the main wing, his motley-following crew behind him, awaiting instruction. He spotted the double doors straight off to the left, and asked a male nurse, "What's through there?"

"Cathy Edwards' room, and the old blocked up wing beyond."

"Cathy Edwards?" piped up Amanda, who could not be persuaded to stay in the safe spaces, and had accompanied Johnny and William. "Is that Ralphie Edwards' mom?"

"Yup," said the nurse. "Been here a long time now."

Jonathan and William gave one another meaningful glances. If Ralphie knew his mom was here – would he have made his way here, too?

On cue, the double doors swung open, and little freckle-faced Ralphie stood there in the darkness of the hallway beyond.

"Well, it looks like we have a welcoming party!" the booming voice of Legion resounded from the little child's pink mouth, horrifying the staff who heard it.

One woman fainted. This was more than she had signed up for, and her mind couldn't take any more.

Jonathan, William and Amanda stood firm.

Behind the little boy, they saw the bespectacled figure of Dr. Henry Cane lurking like a coward. Amanda's stomach lurched, but her resolve held, and she felt an overwhelming power rise within her, an urge to kill such as she had never felt before. Grim faced, her jaw set tight with determination, she took a step forward, gripping the Chinese kitchen hatchet tighter in her hand. Jonathan put a hand on her arm to stop her.

"No," he said firmly, and although her mouth remained clenched, she stopped in her tracks and glared at Henry Cane with pure hatred in her eyes.

"May I be of assistance?" Todd stepped into the group from down the corridor, and smiled. He edged closer to Johnny, staring at him strangely. Amanda took in the blood on his shirt, but what disturbed her more was the smear of blood in the corner of his lips, and the stain around his mouth, as if he had swiped away a great deal of blood with the back of his hand.

"Where's Stan?" she asked.

"Oh, he bought it," Todd shrugged, casually, focusing on Johnny's neck and opening his mouth.

Amanda swooped first, the hatchet singing through the air as she hacked at Todd's neck. He hissed, displaying razor-like incisors and other sharp, shark-like teeth, and she hacked again. Some of the staff, seeing that Amanda had done a good job, came to finish it off.

At the same time, Ralphie leapt forward towards Jonathan, but William stood in the way, and raised his crucifix, attached to his rosary beads.

He held it up and the earth-shaking Legion voice in Ralphie snarled, "You think that I will be afraid of your necklace, boy?"

"EXORCIZO te, immundíssime spíritus, omnis incúrsio adversárii," William intoned clearly, holding the crucifix and rosary beads in one outstretched arm.

Ralphie and Legion gasped, as did Johnny and Amanda. What was Willie doing, and how had he learned to do this?

"Omne phantasma, omnis légio, in nómine Dómini nostri Jesu Christi eradicáre, et effugáre ab hoc plásmate Dei!"

Ralphie stepped back, hissing, but William advanced, closing in on him with the crucifix, still dictating clearly, "Ipse tibi ímperat, qui te de supérnis caeaelórum in inferióra terrae demérgi praecépit. Ipse tibi ímperat, qui mari, ventis et tempestátibus imperávit."

"What the hell, Willie!" gasped Amanda, transfixed. She and Jonathan stepped forward to back him up, not knowing what they could do, but hoping they could help if he needed it.

"Audi ergo, et time, sátana, inimice fidei, hostis géneris humáni, mortis adductor..." Ralphie was whimpering now, alternating that with the curses of Legion within him, as he backed up to where Cathy's door was.

Cathy, half-asleep with a sedative Cane had given her, but driven to action by the maternal instincts within her, was struggling from her bed, and calling, "Ralphie! Ralphie, baby! Come to Momma!"

Ralphie looked around him in panic.

Dr. Henry Cane was nowhere to be seen. A fire door banged at the stub end of the corridor, nearest the partition wall. The coward! He had escaped and left Ralphie and Legion to the mercy of the enemy.

"Jeez," whispered Jonathan, "I know he had Latin lessons at school, and wanted to be a priest, but…"

Legion seethed, unbalanced now and unable to retain the connection, with Cane vanished, Ralphie weakened, and the ghouls apparently all dead – he could feel it in his energy. And his energy was waning.

"Recéde ergo in nómine Patris, et Fílii, et Spíritus Sancti!" said William, punctuating his words with a shake of a small bottle of holy water he produced from a pocket.

Ralphie screamed as if William had poured acid in his face, and a vapour like steam rose from the spots where the water had touched him. He fell to his knees and cried like a child.

Cathy fell forward from her room, and embraced the weeping Ralphie, hugging him to her.

William persisted, "Da locum Spirítui Sancto, per hoc signum sanctæ Crucis Jesu Christi Dómini nostri." He placed the crucifix on Ralphie's forehead and it hissed as if scorching the skin.

Legion bellowed in a wall-shaking roar of anguish and anger.

"Qui cum Patre et eódem Spíritu Sancto vivit et regnat Deus, per ómnia saecula saeculórum!" Jonathan continued, with a flourish. The exorcism was done!

The spirit power of Legion had no choice but to leave Ralphie Edwards' small body, and follow Henry Cane's escape route. He turned white for camouflage reasons in the snowy sky, although he was almost transparent with weakness. He hated white and felt a rising sense of nausea at the symbolic purity of it all. Legion's spirit grew into the huge leather-winged, red-eyed beast. It slowly extended and flapped its white wings testily, feeling the sinuous and bony frame expand and its wings resist the breeze from beneath and the snow from above. It took two thunderous steps forward and raised its taloned claws off the ground. Then it beat its leathery sails of skin powerfully against the breeze, catching the air currents, and shaking the snow-covered trees into mini-avalanches with the force of its beating wings. Rising higher and imperceptibly white in the snowy sky, it swooped over the trees and headed for the obelisk, on the last leg of its journey.

Cathy sat weeping, holding the small body of Ralphie in her arms. At least he had breathed long enough after Legion had left him to smile at her and say, "I love you mommy! Be happy for me now!" Then he died, at last.

"Amen," finished William, and crossed himself. His aunt and old friend Jonathan stood amazed.

"How can you do that? Only priests can perform exorcisms!" gasped Johnny, unable to believe what he'd seen.

"I said I wanted to be a priest," smiled William, "and managed to convince them to fast-track me at the seminary instead of just going to school," he laughed. "Good job I did my exorcism homework, huh?"

The ethereal leather-winged Legion avatar took flight through the snowstorm, foiled on this occasion, but soon his strength would return, with the help of the Cane brothers and he would be able to embody fully, for the End Times.

EPILOGUE

A furious pounding literally shook the ornate oak door practically off the hinges of the McClumpy mansion. Henry Cane angrily sneered at the security camera and stuck out his middle finger to anyone who happened to be watching.

"Aah brother," Talman said jovially, trying to defuse the situation as he opened the door. "It's awfully nice of you to come to clean the snow off my sidewalks! Especially at 2:00 am."

Henry Cane pushed past his brother, never minding he was trudging thick clumps of snow into his brother's foyer and then onto his plush living room carpets as he flung himself onto the nearest couch.

"Tell me Talman, or Josef, or whatever-the-fuck-your-name-is-now, why did Legion decide to attack *my* place of employment!"

"You'll have to ask him that question yourself the next time you chat. It is not my fault that Weston is downstream from Melas. Perhaps it was just coincidence."

"Coincidence my ass!" Henry remarked. "These are modern times, Talman. You cannot just waltz into a fucking hospital and slaughter a bunch of people while another bunch of people watch!"

"I see YOU made it out okay," his brother replied.

"Yes, but that place is a mess. People will be looking for answers. Soon, they'll be looking for me. Wondering where I ran off to."

"Ran off you say?" Talman replied.

"I didn't have a choice. Legion made a real mess of things and I didn't have time to stick around."

"Fret not, dear brother. If you lose your job at Weston, at least you have the part-time gig at the Water Board."

"Fuck off. I like my job at the asylum."

"And I'm sure you'll get things straightened out. You always do."

"That's not all." Henry replied. "The fae has returned."

***

Jeff Abraham had been dead for nearly six hours by the time rescue workers found him. All of the miners had lost their lives on that fateful day when Bridge Creek filled the crevices of the darkened hollows below via the ruptured mine shaft. Jeff, however, was the only body that was ever recovered.

As the ambulance carrying Jeff out of Dark Hollow Road crossed Bridge Creek, the State Police were quick to setup barricades blocking the road from anyone else entering Dark Hollow. The floodwaters had become too dangerous and within an hour later, had covered the bridge itself.

Unbeknown to the county's emergency workers that Jeff would be the only person they would recover, they setup a makeshift morgue and emergency staging area in nearby Melas, waiting uneasily for the waters to subside before returning to their rescue efforts.

This staging area was in the barracks of the West Virginia National Guard. Presently, the barracks looked vacant due to the Guard being dispatched to attend to unseasonable flooding throughout the state.

The body of Jeff Abraham was placed in a black body bag. As soon as authorities could reach his next of kin, they would make proper arrangements to have him sent to a funeral home.

Upstream from Melas was Floyd Lake. Over the past twenty-four hours, water had been steadily pouring over the lake's dam, its water regulation system no longer able to keep up with the ever-increasing water levels. At some point into the night on December 25, the damn broke, sending a torrent of water gushing downstream. Downstream towards Melas.

Although Melas was a ghost town for the most part, the few emergency service workers were immediately evacuated the moment they got word of the dam's collapse. This included evacuating the National Guard barracks and the lone body bag and its contents.

As water gushed through the town, it wasn't long before the makeshift mortuary flooded, taking the body bag downstream. It eventually wound up in Tarklin.

ABOUT THE AUTHOR

Gary Lee Vincent was born in 1974, in Clarksburg, West Virginia, where he lives with his wife Carla and daughter Amber Lee. He is a graduate of Fairmont State University and Columbus University. Vincent holds a Ph.D. and M.S. in Computer Information Systems and a B.S. in Business Administration Management and Psychology.

He is a real estate developer, entrepreneur, author and recording artist.

His interests include music, travel, photography, technology, art, and of course, creative writing.

DARKENED
The West Virginia Vampire Series
Book I – Darkened Hills

A tale of gripping psychological horror!

When evil descends on a small West Virginia town, who will survive?

Jonathan did not start out his life to become a rambler, it just worked out that way. William was a troubled youth with something to hide.

Both were from Melas, a small town tucked away in the West Virginia hills... a town where disappearances are happening more and more frequently.

After the suicide of a wanted serial killer, the townsfolk thought the nightmare was over. But when a centuries-old vampire is discovered they find out the hard way it's just getting started.

Dark secrets can only stay hidden for so long and when the devil comes to collect, there will be hell to pay. Can Jonathan and William find a way to stop the vampire before it's too late? Find out in Darkened Hills!

Paperback.   ISBN: 978-1453844854.

DARKENED
The West Virginia Vampire Series
Book III – Darkened Waters
Coming 2012

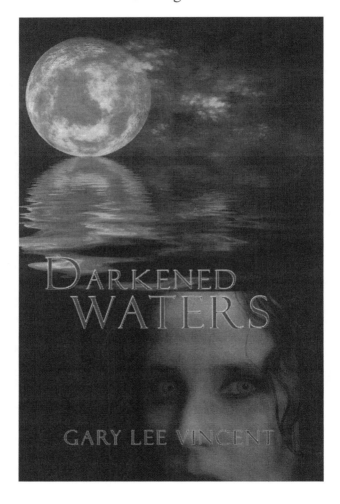

When an archeological dig goes horribly wrong, the team is
trapped in an alternate world where evil awaits them at every
turn. Find out who will survive the *Passageway*! An unforgettable
tale that spans four continents and takes the reader to the very
realm of Hell itself. Part H.P. Lovecraft and part Indiana Jones,
this deadly tale will keep you guessing and wondering which path
to take. Passageway will leave you breathless to the end!

Paperback.   ISBN: 978-1460924785.

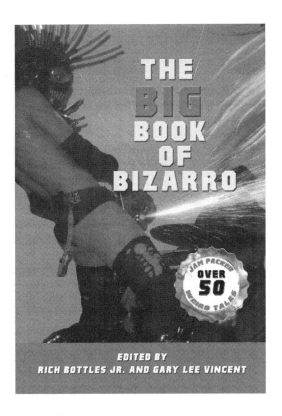

THE BIG BOOK OF BIZARRO

OVER 50

EDITED BY
RICH BOTTLES JR. AND GARY LEE VINCENT

The Big Book of Bizarro brings together the peculiar prose of an international cast of the most grotesquely-gonzo, genre-grinding modern writers who ever put pen to paper (or mouse to pad), including:

NIGHT OF THE LIVING DEAD horror writers John Russo & George Kosana, HUSTLER MAGAZINE erotica contributors Eva Hore, Andrée Lachapelle, & J. Troy Seate and established Bizarro genre authors D. Harlan Wilson, William Pauley III, Laird Long, Richard Godwin and so many more!

From Alien abductions to Zombie sex, *The Big Book of Bizarro* contains OVER FIFTY STORIES of the most outrélandish transgressive fiction that you'll ever lay your capricious and curious hands upon! Paperback. ISBN: 978-0615502038.

Made in the USA
Charleston, SC
16 November 2011